COMING HOME TO MAVERICK

A Christian Cowboy Romance

SOPHIA SUMMERS

Kings Row Press

Chapter 1

Maverick dipped his hat lower against the hot Texas sun. A man's hat could hide a lot of things, unfortunately not everything. His forearms flexed against the rough wood of the split-rail fence, as he stretched his fingers open and closed. His mind was so far away he hardly noticed Colton or the new horse in the small corral used for training horses. This new colt was fighting every effort to break him, and Maverick didn't blame him one bit. He knew his thoughts were ridiculous, but he suddenly wanted that horse on the run, leaping over the fence and taking off across the pasture. Their new trainer was having a devil of a time with the Spawn of Satan, and Maverick wanted to see who would break first—Colton, the trainer, or Spawn, his horse. His bets were on Colton. The horse had passion, fire, and a strong will, exactly what Maverick needed in himself right now.

The tension in the horse's flank, his flared nostrils, and the dance of trainer and horse were familiar, comforting. Maverick imagined himself out there, facing the whip, as he tried to distract himself from the shattering news of a just a few hours ago.

Their property, which stretched for miles in every direction, had always felt like a safe haven. He'd felt God in those hills countless times. But even the stark beauty of the rugged, rocky terrain and rolling green hills couldn't protect him from the news that had sent him out riding the fence line, checking their bales of hay, inspecting the tractors in the back barn, and then finally here to the horse paddock. He'd tried to send some prayers up to Heaven on the way, but at least that afternoon, God was being strangely silent.

His phone rang. "Yeah."

"Where are you?" Dylan's gruff voice made him smile.

"You worried about me?"

"I'm more worried about the paperwork I gotta send to the accountant."

Maverick didn't believe that for a second. "Colton needed some support."

The quiet on the line said more than any response could have. Maverick was hiding. They all knew it.

Maverick grunted. "And I needed some space."

"So you heard."

"How could I not hear when no one can stop talking about it?"

"You coming in for lunch?"

The whole family gathered for lunch every day. It was more like a late breakfast, but it was a family rule that they show up. And for the first time in a long time, Maverick wished he could avoid them, at least for a little while longer. The last time had been when they'd laid their father to rest in the family plot on the northwest corner of their property. His father had been his hero; he'd raised four boys into men, created a successful thriving ranch, and left the Dawson Ranch legacy to Maverick.

And now Maverick's fiancée had returned after six years, with no explanation, no effort to reach out. She just showed back up in their hometown. And he found himself needing some solitude.

Spawn kicked up his back legs and leapt around the paddock, trying to rid himself of the newly placed saddle. Maverick envied the horse. When would it ever be acceptable for Maverick to kick up his heels and buck off whatever he didn't want to deal with?

But he knew he'd best be heading back to the kitchen, or he'd suffer the wrath of Mama. And no one with any sense or brains messed with his mama. He grinned. They owed everything to the strength of that very short woman. "I'll be there."

He heard a grunt of approval or relief or something— who knew what Dylan's grunts meant—and then he hung up the phone. His gaze traveled over the surrounding hills, the patchwork green and tan of the hay they put out every year to feed the livestock. In a couple months, they'd be bringing in the cows to sell at auction. They'd harvest their crops and nestle in for the winter months. The guys would start in on the rodeo circuit, Mama would participate in the local craft shows and fairs, and he'd take a break.

He hopped on the ATV, waved good luck to Colton, who was being controlled by the young horse, and then took the longest path back to the house.

He offered a prayer as he crested the ridge overlooking his family's homestead. "Thank you Lord for all the goodness in our lives, for my brothers and my Mother." He paused, expecting a rush of satisfaction. They'd built something special. The Dawson brothers were known for their cattle, their horses, and their rodeo championships. His father would be proud. They were all fine, honorable men. And according to Dad, that's what mattered. "I don't care what career you choose," he used to say, "but be honest, hardworking, and competent at whatever it is."

Except in Maverick's case, Dad did care what he became. Maverick was the new head of the Dawson Ranch, the new head of the family, as prescribed in the will his father left. Only, Maverick felt like half the man his father had been. He turned the ATV back down the path. His other brothers were pulling up to the house. Time for lunch. He finished his prayer. "I should be grateful, and I am. Help me to show it today even though I've had some hard news." He grit his teeth, knowing he should say the next words, but finding it difficult. "And please bless Bailey. She must have gone through an awful lot. Amen."

A loud, musical horn echoed across the valley, and he shook his head. Nash. Sounded like his youngest brother was in high form. His Jeep spun out in the gravel at the start of the long drive, and then he slowed to a crawl as he approached the house. Maverick nodded to himself. Nash knew better than to throw dust all over Mama's flowers. Mama was continually reminding them that someday they'd have grandkids running around the front yard and they'd all have to be careful.

Grandkids. Maverick had stopped counting how old his kids would have been if he and Bailey had actually been married. They could have had two by then. Or maybe they would have had a long honeymoon relationship with no children. He'd have liked that just as well.

"Stop," he told himself again. Bailey's return to Willow

Creek had brought back emotions he thought he'd buried years ago. But pieces of his heart still longed for her and felt as raw as the day she left. Before he could shut out the memory, the view of the long aisle at the church filled his mind—the pews decorated with ribbons and flowers, the floor sprinkled with flower petals. Everyone they knew and loved smiling up at him, his mother's eyes full of tears, and his father's full of pride. He swallowed the lump in his throat before it could turn into anything that would make his eyes red when he walked into lunch with his family.

He drove down the side of the hill and parked his ATV in the garage, wiping off the trail dust and placing the keys on the hook. Then he went through the workroom, tidying the few items out of place. He brushed the dust off himself again, wiped his face, and ran a hand through his hair. His hat went on a hook—no hats at the dinner table. He was about to open the door into the house when his mama's voice stopped him.

"We love you, son. We'll support you in whatever you want to do."

He turned to face her. Her hair was still damp from her shower, the soft curls framing her face. She stood near the entry into the house, watching him, seeing through his stoic front. Mama was a dear, but she had no notion of the private emotions of a man's heart.

"What I want to do?"

Her eyes were kind with a hint of sorrow, and he hated that he was the cause. She handed him some napkins to bring in from the storage room and a bin for extra dishes.

He'd endlessly analyzed the events of his wedding day and he and Bailey's relationship, and still he couldn't imagine how he could have acted differently. And he didn't

5

know what more he could do now. You can't prepare to be blindsided. And he knew his mama had been hurt in her own way. She'd given her heart to Bailey and had, in some ways, lost a daughter when the woman had left.

Mama nodded. "Yes. We're with you whatever you decide to do—or not do."

He wrapped an arm around her. "I don't know what I want to do. But I do know I love you, Mama. Let's go have some of Cook's food."

She laughed. "The best thing you ever did was hire a cooking staff."

"I see no reason why you have to be the one to make your signature hotcakes."

"Sometimes I go make sure they've got it right," she said with a smile.

"I have no doubt. And they're delicious every time."

She stood on tiptoe. He dipped his head so she could kiss his cheek and give it a pat. "You're a good man, Maverick. You deserve to be happy."

"I am, Mama. What more could a dusty cowpoke need?"

She wiped her hands on the front of her apron and then took it off. She placed it on a hook, and together they entered the house and made their way into the large dining room. Maverick stood in the doorway. All three of his brothers were in town, and each of them sat at the table. Heaping piles of pancakes waited on platters down the center of the table. Almost as much bacon, eggs, toast, and thick slices of ham made his stomach grumble. Instantly, his mood lifted.

"Brothers." He nodded. No one heard him.

Nash stood from his chair. "You can't even go there. If

I'm riding Spice, no one's gonna beat me. Not you, not Tommy, no one."

"You're a mess, Nash."

"Take a look in the mirror before you go making comments, Decker. When's the last time you brought home a first place?"

Mama cleared her throat and nodded toward the sign on the wall behind her. "Dawson happiness starts at home."

The brothers grumbled but closed their mouths.

Mama treated this room as the center of their family. She kept their portraits in there, their senior pictures from high school. The wall also held two phrases the family lived by. "If you're unhappy, get to work" was displayed in large sweeping letters on the opposite wall from the one Mama had just quoted. The brothers stood when Mama entered. She sat at the head of the huge, thick wood table that dominated the room. Then her eyes turned to Maverick, alerting his brothers to his presence.

"Hey, Maverick! How's the colt?" Dylan asked. He was the one who took care of the horses, including their training and breeding.

Maverick felt their eyes on him as he moved to sit at the other end of the table. "He lives up to his name. Good test run for Colton, though you're gonna have to save him. Maybe sooner than later."

Dylan nodded. "He'll come around. They both will. Colton came highly recommended. He has a way with horses like no one I've ever seen."

Maverick was grateful they were talking business. "Nash, I heard your new horn."

"Isn't it awesome!" he said, his grin wide. "I'm taking the Jeep with me when the circuit starts."

"You're going this year?" Mama poured herself some water.

Everyone looked at their mother as Nash nodded. "Of course, I'm going. You said if I finished out two years helping on the ranch, I could spend the next doing the rodeo circuit."

Mama didn't answer. And she avoided Maverick's gaze. If no one else stayed, Maverick was the one who stayed. And so far, he'd been happy with that. He didn't have a problem with taking over for his father; he'd always known some day he would; he'd just thought it would be later. There's nothing else he would rather be doing anyway, he told himself.

Decker, Dylan's twin, usually disagreed with everything Nash said on principle. But he sat quietly, which Maverick found suspicious.

"What are the predictions on the team this year?"

Mama held up a hand. "Wait. Before we get into all that, let's pray."

Everyone waited for Mama to say a few words. "You know I'm proud of you boys. We miss those not with us, your father most of all, but I know he'd be even more proud of every one of you. Thank you for what you give to the ranch. It's a huge endeavor. Your father gave everything he had to this ranch, knowing it would help take care of each of us for as long as we took care of it." Her eyes traveled to each man at the table, and Maverick knew she desperately needed the ranch. He supposed he did too. It was the only thing they had left of their father. If the ranch lived, their father did too. Mama closed her eyes. They held hands around the table and bowed heads.

"Dear Lord bless this family. Bless this land. Bless the

women my boys are going to one day marry. And today especially bless Maverick. We're grateful for every thing in our lives that you placed there in such a perfect way, the hard times and the easy. Amen."

They all echoed, "Amen."

Nash raised his fork. "Let's eat!"

Mama nodded. "Let's eat."

Everyone dug in. Maverick slapped away Decker's hand as he reached for the same slice of ham. "Wait your turn."

Nash passed him a dripping, sticky syrup pitcher.

"Hey now, whoa. Go wipe that off," Maverick said.

"Why me?"

Decker snorted. "'Cause you're the one who drizzled syrup all over the handle."

Nash frowned but got up from the table to wipe the sticky drips of syrup off the handle. The Dawsons had no patience for anything sticky.

They'd almost finished the meal when Decker put down his napkin and looked directly at Maverick. "So, what are you gonna do about Bailey?"

Everyone went silent, and the air thickened with expectation. His mother avoided his eyes, but all three pairs of his brother's eyes waited for his response.

"I don't know that there is anything to do."

"What if she comes walking back in, thinking there's still a chance over here?" Decker's eyes flashed with anger.

"I don't think there's any chance of that. She hasn't said a word to me."

Everyone seemed to be waiting for him to say something else about it. So finally, he sat back in his chair. "I don't know, all right. I had no idea she was coming. I don't know why she left. I don't know what she's been doing except what everyone else knows." He'd stopped checking social media years ago. "So I don't know what to tell you. Will I see her again? I imagine I'll run into her the next time I have to go into town." He tried to keep the pain off his face, but it was just too hard to hide. "I'm not gonna pretend I'm okay with it, but I don't know what else to do except move forward as though we are people that barely know one another."

"We could shun her." Nash twirled his fork. "You know, like outright avoid her, refuse to talk to her. If you asked the town, they'd support you. She hurt them when she left, too." He replaced his fork. "Not as much as you, but they might not want to take her back in with open arms, especially if we say we aren't ready."

Maverick held up his hands. "I don't want us to say or do anything. If we see her, we're polite. If we don't, that's fine too." A part of him wanted to see her right away and get it over with. But the other part wanted to go on a long vacation and hope she left before he came back.

Chapter 2

Bailey stood as tall as she could, but she knew there was no amount of pretending that could help make coming home any easier. She knew word of her arrival had spread through town as soon as her car drove down Center Street.

She hadn't had time or money to change out her obnoxious license plate, *CTRYSTR*. Who put Country Star on their license plate? Bailey had when she left. She shook her head. She hardly knew that woman anymore. But she hardly knew the woman who'd been raised in this town, either. Just the thought of attending church with the members of her town filled her with shame. So why was she back?

She circled around to the other side of the car and opened the door.

"Are we here, Mama?" Gracie Faith's sweet voice warmed her and, at the same time, filled her with anxiety. She reached for her hand. "Come on, sweet pea. Let's go meet your grandma."

And bless her heart, the girl skipped and squealed. Her face alone could have lit the neighborhood.

Oh, please. Please make this easy. It wasn't quite a prayer. She hadn't prayed in a long time. But she sent her plea to the universe anyway. Maybe God still heard people who were afraid to ask Him for things.

They walked up the sidewalk. Everything was the same. The front porch looked like it had a recent paint job. She counted cracks in the old cement, like always. Then she heard a small voice. "One. Two. Three."

She smiled. Willow Creek was the perfect place to grow up. If she could give her daughter even a portion of what Bailey had when she was younger, she'd give her a good place to grow up at last.

Her stomach clenched. Nothing could erase the first five years of her baby girl's life. They were on the road if Bailey was lucky enough to get a gig, and they ate whatever food Bailey could scrape up. How many times had she watched Gracie sleep on a bench at the local bar while Bailey sang on stage?

The door to her parents' farmhouse opened before they made it halfway up the walk. Bailey's mother clutched at her heart, and her face squinched in joy.

"Bailey!" She ran down the stairs and flung her arms around Bailey. Her bony arms held her desperately. She was considerably skinnier since Bailey had seen her last, and the lines in her face were more visible. But she smelled the same. And as Bailey breathed in her mother, everything in her life shifted one degree closer to where things needed to be.

As soon as her mom let her go, Bailey placed a hand on her daughter's head. "And this is Gracie Faith."

Tears welled up in her mother's eyes, and she knelt carefully in front of Gracie Faith. Her loving mother eyes, the same eyes that had so carefully watched over Bailey as a child, searched Gracie Faith's face. "Are you my granddaughter, darling?"

Gracie nodded. "I think so." She reached out and placed a hand on her mama's face. "You look like my mama."

"She's my baby, just like you're her baby."

Gracie nodded. "Then I'm your granddaughter." She said it so matter-of-factly, Bailey wanted to laugh and sob at the intensity of the moment. She'd dreamed how it would be to introduce Gracie to her family since the day her daughter was born.

"I'm so happy to meet you." Bailey's mom smiled. "Do you wanna come inside? I've got cookies, and I can show you your mama's old room. And then we can do whatever you want. I hope you settle right on in and stay awhile." Her gaze flicked to Bailey, and the hopeful love there nearly broke her heart.

"We've come home, Mama. If you've got room, we'd love to stay awhile." She'd called to tell her mother she was coming and that she had a daughter, but nothing could have prepared either of them for this moment.

Her mother's eyes welled up again, and she just nodded. Her dad stood in the doorway.

Her mom stopped. "Look, honey. Bailey's come home."

He stared for a moment. His age had not diminished his broad stature one inch. And then his face broke into a huge smile. "Come here, you." He stretched out his arms and pulled Bailey into the safest place she'd ever known. She broke down and allowed all the tears to fall that she'd been holding in since she arrived in Willow Creek. Tears that she'd been holding in since she'd left in the first place, since she'd found out she was pregnant with this precious new soul. As she quietly shook, hoping not to worry her daughter, her father just hugged her, his hand patting her back.

"Is that Grandpa?" Her daughter sounded concerned, so Bailey backed away, wiping her eyes, and said, "Sweet pea, this right here is the greatest man you'll ever meet. Your grandpa loves you, hon."

She stepped forward and tipped her chin up so she could see his face. "Are you a giant?"

His laugh started deep inside and then bubbled over. "No, I'm no giant, but I sure would like to get to know you."

"I'm Gracie Faith."

"Well, come on in, little nugget. Once we get you settled, I'll take you out to the barn to meet all the other guys we got around here." He stopped. "Let's get you unloaded first." They made their way back to the car, and Bailey bit back her embarrassment. The car gave off an obvious homeless vibe.

"Do you like my bed?" Gracie pointed to her pillow in the back seat. "And Mama sleeps up there when she's not driving."

Her dad choked, his eyes getting misty. It was one of the few times she'd ever seen him get emotional.

"That's nice, Gracie. I love the flowers on your pillowcase."

Gracie grinned as she showed off where they'd been living for the last few months, and Bailey just took it, like she'd known she'd have to. The part of her life she'd hoped to never share with her parents was being put on display. She just kept reminding herself that Gracie was worth it. She deserved a house, a bed, and people who loved her.

Her dad hefted a box onto his shoulder and pulled their one piece of luggage into the house. "Gracie, I can't wait to show you the guys."

"There are more people?"

"He's talking about the horses, love." Mom smiled. "She's gonna go see her room first, dear. And then you can whisk her off to your horses."

"I love horses!" She squealed, and Bailey knew she'd made the right choice in coming home. No matter what it took, she was determined to give her daughter the life she deserved.

When they walked into Bailey's old room, she about doubled over as her stomach clenched in pain. Pictures of her and Maverick were everywhere. The morning she'd spent getting ready for her wedding flashed before her eyes. Nothing in the room had changed. Her hairbrush was right where she'd left it. Her makeup case. The perfume she'd worn that day. She leaned against the doorframe, hoping no one else noticed how shaken she felt. She watched her daughter run around the room, picking up old rodeo trophies, hugging stuffed animals. And then when Gracie climbed up into the large four-poster, Bailey let the tears fall. Her attention drifted to the window overlooking the back pasture. She'd always stood at that window to watch the horses.

"Chester?" Her voice caught in her throat.

"Daddy couldn't sell her. She's out there whenever you're ready."

Her body literally itched to go take a ride, but she had

to get Gracie settled first. Tonight, after everyone was in bed, she'd go talk to her horse.

Once they were all settled and Grandpa was showing Gracie how to brush down the horses, Bailey sat with her mom on the porch that overlooked the back paddock and pasture. "You and Dad look great."

"We're blessed with good health. But he's slowing down, only working horses for our friends now. I'm happy at the county fair now and then. Otherwise, we lead a quiet life."

Her mother didn't ask where she'd been. She had to have a million questions, but she didn't ask a single one. She just waited.

"I'm happy to be home. Do you mind if I...stay awhile?"

Her mom's hand reached for hers and squeezed. "You can stay as long as you like. You and your daughter are always welcome."

"Thanks, Mom." Her throat felt tight again. They had a lifetime, she hoped, to talk about what had happened, about why she hadn't been able to face them with her poor choices. How did one own up to leaving her fiancé at the altar? And then living with another man, having his baby, getting thrown out with nowhere to go, and utterly failing in every area of her life? She didn't know. And so she never had. It had taken every bit of grit she had left to come home. And now that she'd returned, it was enough to just sit at her mom's side.

As she exhaled slowly and let the remaining tension leave her body, she thought about the last time she'd sat on this porch.

With Maverick.

His strong hand had covered both of hers. "I'm always here for you. That's what forever is all about."

She hadn't believed him. She felt sure that if she told him she wanted to explore her music before getting married, that she was suffocating in their small town, yearning for space, for freedom, that he would give up on her. Everyone wanted to marry Maverick Dawson. The Dawson brothers were where life started and stopped in this town.

Another sigh escaped before she could stifle it.

"He's still single, you know."

"I know." She wasn't even surprised her mama knew what she was thinking. But she didn't want to think about Maverick. Not yet.

Dad and Gracie walked toward them, hand in hand.

"She's such a beautiful child, and she has a good heart. You can see it in her eyes."

"She really is, Mama. She's something special. I just want to give her what I had."

"I'm so happy to be in her life. I didn't even know…" She reached for Bailey's hand again. "Sorry. You had your reasons, and I trust that."

Bailey just nodded. "I'll talk about it when I can. I—I'm sorry." Her voice broke, and she looked away.

"No, no, honey. I'm just here to love on you. That's all that's needed right now."

Gracie bounded up the stairs and threw her arms around Bailey. "Mama! You should see the horses! Grandpa said he'd teach me to ride! He has the prettiest pony. Can I, Mama? Please?"

Bailey's eyes welled with tears again. "Of course, darling. That's why we're home."

Long after Gracie was in bed, Bailey sat on a couch in the living room, curled up with a blanket, a book in her lap. "I miss Red." Her golden retriever had never left her side when she was home. She loved that dog. He had known all her secrets and took them to his grave while she was gone.

Her dad sat up. "Gracie Faith needs a dog."

Her mom was about to shake her head, but Dad held up a finger. "No child can grow up without a dog to love her."

"You guys don't have to get a dog," Bailey said.

"Of course, we do. I'll take her to the shelter tomorrow. If there's not a good one for kids, we'll look around for puppy announcements. Someone's always trying to get rid of some of their litter around here."

Bailey didn't have the heart to argue. Her parents loved to help and wanted nothing more than to do nice things for her and her daughter. She'd been blessed well beyond what she deserved. "I don't think she's gonna know what to do with herself. First grandparents, then horses, and now a pet dog." She pulled the blanket up tighter around her even though she wasn't cold. "Thank you."

Her dad chuckled. "Well now, there's no thanking us."

"Yes, honey. We love you. You know that." Her mother's words were comforting, but her eyes held a hint of insecurity that Bailey wished she'd never put there.

"I need to tell you guys why I left."

Dad held up his hand. "When you're ready. We trust you."

"Thank you. I'm not even sure I know, really. I was...I was thinking about marriage to Maverick, about living here my whole life, about all my dreams of singing and going to

Nashville—you know how when I was a little girl I used to go out back and sing to the orchard?"

"That's where it all started." Her mom smiled. "And then at church and in the county fair."

"Well, over time I realized that wasn't enough, but I never told anybody. I figured I had a good life, a good man, a good future. I should be happy. But I'd never been anywhere. College was only an hour away, and Maverick was my only boyfriend." She closed her eyes and leaned her head back.

"Nobody knew you weren't happy."

"I don't even know if *I* knew I was unhappy. That's the thing. I didn't know myself at all. And I got scared and took off for Nashville. What I did was so terrible that I didn't dare contact you, and then it became easier not to—and then it became too long of a time I'd let slip by." She forced herself to meet their eyes. "I was living a life I now you don't approve of. And then Gracie…"

"Sounds like you're well on your way to figuring things out," her dad said.

Bailey smiled ruefully. "Hopefully I can figure it out before I have to talk to Maverick."

"Everybody makes mistakes. It's been five years. He's a good man."

"You'll feel better when you do," her mom urged.

"I know I was unhappy, and I needed to communicate better, but what I lacked most of all was gratitude and courage. And for that, I'm so sorry. I'm sorry I left without telling you and that I didn't talk to you all these years." She swallowed. "I know that's not good enough, just saying sorry when you do something that big, that hurtful. It's gonna take some time for you to forgive me. But I'll make it up to you, pay you back, work the ranch. I'll prove again that I can be the daughter you deserve."

"Oh, honey, no." Her mom jumped up and sat as close as she could to Bailey. "That's not how it works with us. And that's not how it works with God either. You keep talking to Him. He'll let you know. And as far as your Daddy and me, we forgave you years ago."

"Oh, I don't talk to Him any more. How can I when I let everyone down like I did? Maverick...." She shook her head. "I just don't think God wants to hear much from me anymore."

"Well, it's times like this when you need to talk to Him the most. He's way better than your Daddy or I am about forgiving." She patted her knee. "Honey, there is nothing ever that can separate you from the love of our Lord."

"That's the absolute truth. You can read that in Romans eight if you want to remember." Her dad shook his head. "Don't you worry about us. Just like your Mother said, we've already forgiven you. Long time ago."

She nodded, but she didn't know what to say. She would do whatever she could to help these parents of hers who deserved so much. But she didn't think she could ever make it right with Jesus, not after all she'd done. "I wish I had come back years ago."

"Looked like you were kind of busy."

"Singing in some local places."

Bailey started. "What? Did you come?"

"Did we come? Your mother made a book."

"She did?" Bailey was shocked when Mom brought out a thick three-ring binder packed with pages and handed it to her. Her lap felt weighed down with the pages.

"We started this as a wedding gift."

The first page was a double spread of her and Maverick as kids—their elementary school pictures and others. She skipped ahead, grazing past the pre-wedding shots, the bridals, the engagements. And then she stopped at a pair of tickets to her first gig and a picture of her parents standing together in front of the venue.

"You were there?" She couldn't stop the tears. They were too kind. "You were there?" Had they tried to come see her backstage? Had security bounced them out? Had they just watched and left? She couldn't handle the answers to those questions, so she set the binder aside. "I'm sorry. I didn't even know." She stood, not even able to stand her own self. "I think I need time to let this settle. Can I look at it later?"

"Of course." Mom shut the book as Bailey hurried from the room, choking back sobs.

When she was back in the guest room, she dried her tears and lay back in her bed. As she tried to drift off to sleep, Maverick's face came into her mind. She'd grown up with him. They had memories from every year of her life until she'd left. But the face she saw now was not the childhood Maverick but the man who'd loved her. The man who had cupped her cheeks in his large, rough hands and kissed her softly, tenderly, over and over until she didn't know what to do with the yearning that swelled up inside. That's the Maverick that lulled her to sleep as she hugged a pillow and wished she didn't have to tell him what she'd done.

Chapter 3

Maverick rode out over his property on his favorite horse, flying over the hedges, tearing across meadows, and pushing Thunder to his limit. The horse loved it. Maverick could feel the power and rhythm beneath him, feel the shuddering flanks under his calves, sense the horse's desire to break free and push himself to his limits.

Thunder knew where they were going. He'd known before Maverick knew. And once Maverick realized Thunder was heading to the ridge, he didn't try to stop him.

The ridge—the property line between his land and Bailey's. It had been their meeting spot for all the years he'd known her. A huge climbing tree dominated the area, which they'd climbed as children and sat beneath as youth. He'd first thoroughly explored what it meant to kiss Bailey under that tree. If Maverick thought hard enough, he could still remember the feel of her mouth. As Thunder reached the final stretch of the climb, Maverick hopped off and let him wander. There was a stream nearby for water, and Thunder could graze on the grass down the other side. Without even planning to, Maverick went to stand on the ridge and stared down into Bailey's property.

He'd come here almost every day for months after she'd left, staring down into her fields. Sometimes he'd watch the horses run. Her father used to breed and train them like the Dawson Ranch did. He'd sold off many—some of which Maverick had purchased—and now kept a modest group in his retirement. Bailey's parents had been like second parents to him, and he'd turned to her father when his own had died.

He looked away from the view. Bailey hadn't come to the funeral. Not even a phone call. He'd heard talk that she'd been singing in bars, and he'd tried to contact her. Even if he could have only heard her voice, he might have felt better, gotten some answers, but his calls never reached her. And now, before she'd returned, he thought he'd forgiven her, thought that he was over her, but news of her arrival brought back intense feelings—even anger. A fire raged through him as he relived it all again. He'd give himself this one luxury one more time—he clenched his fists—then he would conquer this.

The sound of a horse running toward him pounded through his heart, and he knew it had to be Bailey. He whistled for Thunder. The last thing he wanted was to see the woman who had left him at the altar, who hadn't spoken a word to him since, and who had suddenly showed back up in his town to disturb his peace. His heart ached in a twisted, anger-filled fear at having to face her. Not right now. Not like this.

Thunder came running toward him, and he swung his leg up, turning the horse to take off down his side of the ridge.

But just then, Bailey soared over the top, coming down right on top of him. Midair, she screamed, her eyes wide.

Thunder bucked and kicked before Maverick could get him to move out of the way. Bailey pivoted and landed so close he felt her. And then Thunder burst forward, taking him far away from the ridge and Bailey. Maverick considered letting him run. Thunder's startled speed would be enough to carry him away down the valley and back home, but that would be cowardly and ridiculous. Her horse whinnied. With years of Dawson training behind him, he pivoted and returned to her side.

Her horse hobbled. She jumped off and reached for his ankles. "Whoa, boy." Her soft, husky voice shivered through Maverick. And his reaction to her irritated him. It reminded him of all the reasons why she had no business being back in his life. But if he didn't intervene, she was gonna get herself knocked over by her injured horse...or kicked in the head.

"Stop." He walked forward, approaching the horse slowly. The horse reached for a friendly nuzzle into Maverick's chest. He rubbed him on the forehead, whispering calming sounds. After a moment, when he knew the horse was calm, he nodded. "Now, let's take a look at you."

"I already did that. It's a sprain."

"Did you go to veterinary school while you were gone? 'Cause last I checked, you were not the expert here."

She huffed. "You don't have to be an expert to spot a sprained ankle."

He walked around the horse until he was standing over

Bailey while she crouched down by the horse's feet. He spoke to the top of her head. "Could you move around front and talk to him while I take a look?"

Their eyes met, and hers widened before she looked away. Then she nodded.

He patted the horse's side, letting him know he was down there, and then gingerly felt along the bones and tendons and muscles. His flank shivered in pain when Maverick touched a soft spot. Maverick stood, irritated Bailey was right. "We'll have to walk him back."

She folded her arms across her chest, her eyes fiery with challenge—he used to love when she looked at him like that. Sometimes he'd tease her relentlessly just to see her want to lay into him. He looked away, the memory too pleasant for his mood.

"Come on." He reached for Thunder's lead and started walking back toward the ridge. Before he descended toward her family's house, he looked back over his shoulder. "You coming?"

"Just like that?"

"Just like what?"

"You think you can step in to help and be back in my life just like that?"

He shook his head. "I didn't say anything about wanting to be back in your life."

Her hurt was so obvious he regretted his words, but it was only the truth. He'd learned his lesson with her and suffered for years because of it.

"I don't need you to walk me home. We're not fifteen."

"Well, I can't let you go alone. You're gonna need some help if he turns his ankle on a rock or something."

She held up her phone. "I've got a phone."

"And what would your parents say if they knew I just let you go by yourself?"

"So this is for them?"

"It's what nice people do when someone needs help. Or have you been gone from Willow Creek too long to remember?"

"I guess so." She led her horse carefully and proceeded to ignore him.

He walked along, kicking up dirt as he went. The area was dryer than usual, with no rain for almost a full season. It had been a strain on the ranch, and their hay crop had suffered. None of which she would know since she hadn't bothered to reach out even once.

The further they went, the angrier he became. And all the questions, the years of waiting, the wishing for a chance to simply talk to her again was catching up to him. Before they'd walked halfway to her house, he was biting his tongue to keep his frustration from flowing out of him. So much snark rose to the surface he surprised even himself. *Wouldn't have hurt you to text once in a while. Or did you lose your phone for five years?*

Then he heard a sniff.

She was crying.

His anger melted. No way was he gonna let go of years of pain, but crying was too much. "What's the matter?"

She sucked in her breath, but he didn't turn around. They were walking single file, and he needed to watch his feet placement carefully.

"Are you hurt?" he asked.

"No."

They continued down the path, and now he was

plagued with curiosity, with compassion, and, yes, with anger. But it was so much more complicated than the righteous anger he'd felt.

And she was still silent. He shouldn't even be surprised.

They finally reached the flat pastureland of her family's property.

"I can make it fine from here. You can get back to the ranch."

"Nah, I'll come in and say hello to your parents."

She groaned, and he couldn't understand her problem.

He whirled around to face her. "What? You don't want me around?"

She stepped back, startled. Her expression was guarded, worried. "No, it's not that. I…" She waved her hand in the air. "It's nothing. Come on in. My parents would be thrilled to see you."

He shook his head. This was too much. He kicked at a rock. "You know, you owe me some answers."

She waited half the length of the pasture to respond, but then her quiet "I know" warmed him. With relief, he realized she wasn't going to leave him in the dark forever.

As soon as they made it to the back porch, a little girl slammed open the back door. She tore across the grass toward Bailey, who swung her into her arms and kissed her cheek. "How's my sweet pea?"

Maverick couldn't have been more surprised if she'd come out of his own house.

"So good! Grandma taught me how to make cookies and her special bread."

"What! *I* don't even know how to make her supersecret, special bread."

"You don't?" Her awe made Maverick chuckle. She turned to him, her blue eyes blazing. "Who are you?"

"Gracie. Manners, remember?"

"Oh, sorry." She held out her hand. "Hello. I'm Gracie Faith."

He laughed out loud at that and shook her hand. "Well, Gracie Faith, I'm Maverick Dawson. Pleased to meet such a pretty little kitchen helper."

"I help with the horses too." She wiggled out of Bailey's arms and went running back up onto the porch and into the house. "Grandpa! Mama's brought home a Maverick."

Maverick whipped his head around. "Mama?" His heart about stuttered to a stop.

Her eyes widened, and she searched his face before turning toward the barn. "Let's put the horses away and wrap this one's ankle."

He wasn't sure how, but he managed to put one foot in front of the other all the way to the barn. Bailey had a daughter? How was that possible? "How old is she?"

Bailey shook her head. "Let's talk about it inside."

Mr. Hempstead called from the porch behind them, "Good to see you, Maverick."

He turned. "You too, Mr. Hempstead."

"Is Chester limping?"

Bailey called, "Yeah, it's a sprain."

"Get Maverick to wrap it for us, will you? I'll take a look later."

Maverick didn't hide his personal satisfaction that Mr. Hempstead wanted him to wrap it. They turned Thunder loose in the paddock and walked Chester to a stall.

They worked together in silence with an ease that came

naturally even after all these years. He reached for the gauze while she was handing it to him. She was about to lift the hoof when he did it for her.

When Maverick shut the door, sliding the latch, they both turned from Chester's stall, and he asked the first question of many. "So…"

"Oh, stop, Maverick. This is hard enough as it is."

He was taken aback by the agony in her voice. "I'll try to be more sensitive, but you have to realize you're not the only victim here."

Her eyes softened, and then she sat on a bench just inside the barn door. "I love the smell in here."

"I do too." He sat beside her and waited. Minutes passed before he turned to eye her. "You wanna tell me what is going on here?"

"No."

"Bailey, come on."

"I'm sorry. I wasn't expecting to see you yet. I imagined all of this differently."

He waited.

"You'll lose whatever respect you have left for me."

He tipped his head and searched her face, still saying nothing.

"She's mine. Her name's Gracie Faith. She's a perfect angel and the best thing that's ever happened to me. But she deserves better than what I've been giving her, so I came home. Mom and Dad raised me right. I know they can help me do good by her as well." Her gaze flicked to his and then away again just as quickly.

"And how old is she?"

"Five."

"Five? You left six years ago. Is she—she's obviously not mine." The words left a bitter feeling on his tongue.

"No, she's not yours, Maverick." Her voice sounded small, scared.

About four hundred emotions hammered through him at once. They'd planned to wait until they were married for their intimacy to progress to that point. So was he grateful that the child wasn't his? No, not exactly. The longer he sat beside Bailey, the more betrayed he felt. When he allowed himself to imagine that she'd broken their vow, that she'd been with another man when they'd had so many almost moments together, he was fired up with burning jealousy, resentment, and...desire. A part of him wished that the child was theirs, that Bailey had stayed and married him like she'd said she would.

He didn't know what to do with himself. He stood up and walked to the door.

"Maverick?" Her small voice only irritated him further. He waved her away, not trusting himself to speak.

"You just gonna stand there?"

He nodded. He flexed his hands, took a step, then stopped and turned, so many words tumbling through his thoughts, so many accusations. "I have to go." He stepped out of the barn and whistled for Thunder.

"That's all you have to say?"

He stopped and tilted his head, rotating his neck on his shoulders. "Nope."

"Then just say it, Maverick."

Thunder scooted to a stop at the paddock's gate. Maverick opened it and hopped on his horse. Then he tipped his hat in her direction. "You first."

She stepped back and nodded. "Fair enough."

He tapped Thunder's side. The horse was only too ready to take off back up the ridge. Thunder flew across her property, up the hill toward their tree. As Thunder leapt over the ridge and tore through the pastures back to his barn, Maverick knew he wouldn't be feeling better any time soon.

Chapter 4

Bailey paced in the barn long after Maverick left. He'd changed in some ways, but he was still the same Maverick, the man who could drive her crazy with desire. He was the good one, the smart one, the responsible one. He was always the one everyone in town looked to.

If she had a problem, he swooped in and solved it. Only, this time, he might be just as much of a mess as she was. He'd barely kept his anger reined in. This volatile side of Maverick was completely new. And there was a strange desperation in his eyes. Where he had once approached the world like it was a tool in his hands, he now waited with worry for what might happen next. She could see the vulnerability in his face.

She'd done that to him. If he never forgave her, she wouldn't blame him one bit.

She'd tried life without him, and she couldn't hack it. And here she was, dragging her sorry butt back to Willow Creek. She squeezed her eyes closed so tight she thought her eyelashes would break. Facing her guilt for all the wrong she'd done to Maverick was too much. Running and pretending like it had never happened had been easy, in a horribly hard kind of way. She'd never have come back if not for Gracie Faith. And she couldn't run forever. And hiding didn't make anything right. The small part of her heart that remembered Sunday School told her that. She needed to make things right.

When she thought of how happy her little girl was with her mom and dad, being loved on from every direction, safe, with enough food to eat, she knew she'd made a good choice.

But those weren't the only reasons she'd come. She owed some major explanations to Maverick. A part of her hoped that there was the tiniest chance he would forgive her. She had no hopes they'd get back together, not with Gracie Faith in the picture. He might try to step in and help them, but she didn't want to be another project for Maverick Dawson.

She wanted his friendship, but only if he wanted to be in her life, not because he felt sorry for her. And maybe, just maybe, if he forgave, her, God might too. She shuddered, thinking of all she'd done that was wrong. And not just wrong for her, wrong for her little girl. How did that work with God? She couldn't make these five years right. She couldn't make it right that she'd given Gracie a man who didn't care about them for a Daddy. She closed her eyes against her thoughts, pushing them into their familiar place in her brain, far far away.

When she went back into the house, her parents' gaze followed her, but she said nothing. They finished up the evening saying very little. Even Gracie noticed and played quietly in her room. The air felt heavy, and only her determination to stay in Willow Creek for Gracie's sake kept Bailey from running.

The next day, they woke early to head over to the fairgrounds. Bailey caught some excitement from Gracie. Her daughter had never seen a county fair. And especially not a Texas county fair. Bailey grinned. "We are gonna have to see what they're deep-frying this year."

"What's deep-fry?"

Her own child didn't know what a fair deep-fry was. "Oh, it's a special way of cooking things, and every year, they deep-fry something unusual, and that's what makes it exciting."

"Unusual? Like what?"

Bailey had to wrack her brain for some crazy examples. "Well, like there's always deep-fried bacon. Or one year, it was Twinkies. I didn't much care for peanut butter sandwiches deep-fried, but the pickles were good."

Gracie's nose wrinkled. And Bailey had to laugh. Gracie was the least adventurous eater she'd ever heard of. "Don't worry. Deep-frying makes everything taste good."

"Really?"

"That's what Grandpa says."

"Okay, then I'm gonna try it."

When they walked in through the front gates, Gracie was still talking about it. And while Bailey was laughing with her about the possibility of deep-fried popsicles, they ran into one of the Dawson brothers. They stumbled and almost tripped over themselves. Not the impression Bailey was going for in front of the Dawson clan.

He held his hands out to steady them both. "Whoa now, ladies. Are you all right?" His eyes swept over them both in a friendly manner.

"Yes, thank you." She squinted her eyes and studied him. "You're a Dawson, and I know it's been a while…"

He tipped his hat. "Yes, ma'am."

"Nash?"

"The very one. And now I'm going to have to know your name."

"Nash, it has been too long if we don't recognize each other. I'm Bailey, and this is my daughter, Gracie Faith."

His eyes widened, but to his credit, that was the only response he gave to what must have been astonishing news. "Well now, it's good to see you again, Bailey."

Gracie smiled at him. "I like your name. Nash." She tested it out in her mouth. "Naa-aash."

He tipped his head, giving a signature Dawson smile. "And now I like it even better. Thank you for letting me know."

"I knew Nash when he was a little boy just as old as you are. The last time I saw him, he was in high school." She eyed him, standing above them, as broad as his brothers. "And much smaller."

"You used to be little like me?" Gracie's head was tipped all the way back, looking up into his face.

"I can't remember such a thing, but if your mama says it's true, then I believe her."

At his kind words, Bailey felt everything in the world ease up a bit. "Thank you, Nash. Where you headed?"

"I was going to head toward home. But now I'm going to turn around and head back in with you ladies."

"Oh, you don't have to…"

"If I didn't, Mama would put me on barn mucking duty. You know how she feels about things like this."

"I do. The Dawson brothers are all about obligations."

"Well now, I don't know if our family policy deserves that bitter tone. It's not like you and my brother don't have a history or anything." The way he said *history* and wiggled his hands in the air made her laugh.

"Oh, fine. Come on, then."

They made their way to the entrance, and Bailey tried not to notice how everyone around them was taking an extra interest.

As soon as she stepped inside the fairgrounds, a rush of nostalgia made her smile. "Now, this is what I've been missing!"

"There you go!" Nash sauntered like every cowboy should. "Nothing like a county fair."

"Any of you boys riding today?"

"You know we are. Me and Decker for sure." He leaned closer. "And don't tell now, but they're trying to get Maverick back on a bull to do his signature move."

"The move! I'd forgotten the move." Everything about home was just the same. Except that it wasn't. Maybe for an afternoon, she could forget her mistakes and the mess she'd made of her life and enjoy the fair with her daughter.

Gracie ran up to a small corral full of baby pigs. "Oh, Mama! Would Grandpa buy me a pig too?"

"She already knows who to ask! Smart girl." Nash tipped his hat to her.

"Thanks. She really is special."

Gracie stretched her hand through the fence to touch a piglet on the head and giggled.

Food trucks filled the air around them with delicious smells, smells that brought back memories of her mother's quilting booth and pie tables. Memories of long glorious days with friends, searching every inch of the county fair park. And memories of Maverick and stolen kisses in the horse stalls.

"Might I get you two ladies a frozen lemonade?" Nash was all charm, all politeness, and Bailey had forgotten how nice it was to be around someone who worked to put you at ease.

Another tall and broad Dawson waved as he approached. "Nash! Who do we have here?" Decker's twin, Dylan, was soon at his side, and Bailey was surrounded by Dawson testosterone.

She laughed. "Hey, guys! It's great to see you all."

Decker, Dylan, and Nash towered above her. Their broad shoulders and immense size were offset by the signature Dawson twinkle in their eyes. She was transported back to her high school days for a minute until a small hand tugged at her shirt. "Mama?" Gracie's small voice sounded unsure.

"Oh, honey. I want you to meet some more friends." She swung her up into her arms. "Remember Maverick?"

She nodded.

"Well, these are his brothers."

"Oh." She wiggled to be lowered to the ground so Bailey set her on her toes.

Nash got down on his knee. "You already know me. Isn't that right?"

She nodded. "You're the little one."

The other guys snorted.

"That's right." Nash waved them off. "Well now, these guys are just a bunch more like me."

She considered him a minute and then lifted her eyes all the way up to the tallest.

Decker winked. "Nice to meet you."

"You too." Gracie seemed to rally. "Grandpa's gonna buy me a pig."

"Is he now?"

A crowd of elementary school kids approached. "Oh, pig," someone called from behind them.

A large group of full-grown pigs were walking down the dirt path toward them with the children right behind.

Gracie squealed. "Look!"

"Oh, fun. It's the 4-H kids." Bailey laughed. "Remember when we did that?"

"Yeah, we remember." Decker frowned.

"Oh, let it go." Dylan shook his head. "Still chapped your pig lost?"

"It can't be my fault it rolled in dirt."

"It's the pig's fault, then, but the pig also lost. Time to get over it."

Bailey thought about all the hours she'd spent on her pig, training it, feeding it, bathing it. At the time, she'd outgrown the initial excitement, and it felt more like a chore than anything; but looking back, those were some of her happiest memories. Gracie's gaze was glued to the young children as they walked by, calling commands to their pigs, tapping their shoulders, and the pigs moved along accordingly. Bailey knew her next question before she asked.

"Mama."

"Yes, sweet pea."

"Could I have my own pig to boss like those guys?"

"Someday, baby girl."

Her lip stuck out, but she didn't say anything else.

The 4-H group rounded the next corner. And then Nash returned with frozen lemonade.

They walked along, all the brothers still at her side. "Don't you guys have something to do?"

Dylan shrugged. "Nope."

Decker shook his head.

Nash lifted his hat to wink at Bailey. "Anybody else feel like Bailey's trying to get rid of us?"

"A little bit." Decker raised a finger. "I'm getting that vibe."

"Oh stop. Let's go say hello to my mom." Bailey's mom sat in the same spot she always had, with shelves and baking racks behind her, along with a tall image of a pie fresh from the oven and her signature logo for Patty's Pies.

"And now Bailey will learn the real reason we're hanging around." Nash winked and then approached her mom's pie booth. "Well now, hello, Mrs. Hempstead. Don't you look lovely today."

She laughed and beckoned him closer. "I've been saving this piece right here for you."

Nash reached for the slice of her mom's boysenberry pie and grabbed a fork. "Now this here is why I come to the fair."

Decker closed in. "I want a taste of why *I* come to the fair."

Her mom handed him a slice of the blueberry.

And Dylan got the strawberry. "I think she saved the best one for me."

"Nah, we all know Maverick gets that one." Nash glanced quickly at Bailey and then back at her mom.

Bailey checked her watch. "I think it's time for the bird show."

Decker nodded. "And we've got to get in costume."

"We'll come see you." Bailey waved to them as the twins ran off.

Nash pointed at Gracie. "I'll be looking for you, little lady."

She grinned and stuck the straw to her lemonade back in her mouth.

As soon as they'd all left, Gracie said, "Who were all those tall guys?"

"I told you. They're Maverick's brothers. My friends." Her heart ached when she said it. They were really like brothers to her. They would have been her brothers. But now they were friends, and that would have to be good enough.

She knew that coming home was going to be full of the bittersweet, just like a bar of rich, dark chocolate. Hopefully it stayed decadent, and she could work through the moments that tore at her heart.

Chapter 5

Maverick stood as far back as he could, watching the cozy picture in front of him. Bailey was walking through the fairgrounds with her beautiful girl skipping at her side. They were laughing. Gracie would point to things, and then Bailey would excitedly say something. He'd seen the pair surrounded by his brothers, and for a moment, everything in the world seemed right. At last, Bailey was home.

But then the reality of their situation left him in screeching pain. She'd left. She didn't want him in her life —she didn't want to live in this town.

Then why was she back? He tried to hang on to the old familiar bitterness so he didn't run over to her and drool all over the scene like an excited puppy. But he couldn't help the nostalgia that crept into his heart. If he and Bailey had married, that could have been *their* little girl. That could have been *his* life. As he watched them, he couldn't help but wonder what was keeping him from scooping up all that happiness for himself. Why not let go and try again?

He could think of a few reasons that kept him back

where he was, watching instead of standing at their side. But then Gracie tugged on her mom's hand and dragged her over to the mechanical bull. That clinched it.

Maverick jogged over. Gracie wanted to ride, but Bailey was shaking her head. The man at the front of the line got on, and the bull started rocking back and forth.

Gracie jumped up and down, clapping.

Then the bull picked up the pace, and the man fell to the ground.

Gracie frowned and paused. And Maverick couldn't let that be. No daughter of Bailey's was gonna be afraid to get up on a mechanical bull. Maverick flexed his fingers and rotated his shoulders, then he crouched down beside her. "You know, Gracie, your mom can stay on one of these longer than anyone I know."

"Used to." Bailey shook her head. "And the final Dawson brother has arrived."

"You already saw my brothers?"

"Yep, you missed boysenberry pie."

"Oh no, ma'am. I never miss boysenberry pie. Your mama is good enough to save me a piece. Every time." He couldn't tell if she was pleased or irritated to learn he was on close terms with her parents.

"Excuse me, Uncle Maverick?"

"Yes, sweet pea." He loved her small voice. And "Uncle Maverick" was a definite improvement.

"Can my mama really ride the bull?"

"She's so good at it. One of the best."

"Oh, Mama. I wanna see!"

Bailey eyed him for long enough that Maverick almost lost hope, and then with one last look at her daughter, she nodded. "I will, but only if Maverick does it too."

"Oh yes! You should both ride!"

"I could, little lady, but then I might beat your mama, and she doesn't like that much."

Gracie puckered her forehead and pressed her lips together, thinking about their dilemma for so long that he wanted to scoop her up and swing her up onto his shoulders. She was just so dang cute. Then she said, "I think you should ride together."

And she won all of his gratitude, because the deep red on Bailey's face was worth whatever awkwardness came after.

He tipped his head back and laughed. "You know, there was one time we did."

Bailey's horrified expression made him laugh even harder. "Maverick, this is not the time…"

He held up his hand. "It's the truth." People nearby were now listening, and he turned to look at them. "Maybe some of y'all remember?" He paused, but no one seemed to know what he was talking about. "You know, the time when Bailey and I rode the bull together."

Low chuckles followed, and Bailey looked like she wanted to hide.

"Do it again!" Gracie clapped her hands and stepped up on the split-rail fence that circled the bull.

Bailey shook her head. "We're not riding that thing together, Maverick." She handed him her purse, paid the guy, and stepped up into the stirrup.

Watching her swing her lithe, strong body up on that bull did things to Maverick, things that he didn't want to resist. She was just the kind of woman he'd always loved. She was the only woman he'd ever loved. And if looking at her was gonna get his blood boiling, that was just the way of things. So he let his eyes glide over her, and he welcomed the deep emotion that came with it. He'd always loved the way Bailey looked, but what he really loved about Bailey was the fire that burned inside. And that was on full display right now too.

He sidled up next to Gracie. "Your mama is something special, you know that?"

She nodded. "Yup. She's a star."

"Well now, that might be true. But that's not what I'm talking about. Your mama has special mom magic. She's smart. And good to other people, and super fun. She'd drop everything to help a friend, and you're lucky to have her, of all the women in the world, as your mom."

Gracie's eyes widened, and she watched her mom with a new sparkle.

Bailey looked between them, and Maverick couldn't get a read on her expression. She waved to them. "Okay. Gracie, honey, this is for you. 'Cause there's no way I'd be up here for any other reason than to show my little girl that women can do this too."

Maverick tipped his hat. "You're not gonna hear any argument from me."

Bailey nodded to the guy running the ride, and it started to move. The ride began slow, the rocking motion easy to move into as you adjust your body to the swaying and dipping. But most riders still fell off in the first twenty seconds anyway. If you made it through the easy stuff, then the bull started jerking and hopping and rotating in full circles, and it became truly difficult to stay on, even for Maverick.

The longer Bailey went, the larger the crowd grew. Gracie clapped. "Go, Mommy!"

And on she went. One minute. One minute thirty. A large horn blared, alerting everyone that she'd broken the record. And Bailey kept at it.

The bull dipped low, rose up, and jerked to the side at the last minute, flinging her to the ground.

Bailey stood up, brushing off the hay and the dust. She walked toward them, looking a little shaky.

Maverick rushed to her side. "Hey, you all right?"

She nodded. "Dizzy," she whispered, then she reached for her girl. "What did you think?"

Gracie clapped. "The record! You beat it! Did you hear? I think there's no way anyone's gonna beat that."

"Oh yeah? Maverick has to try, remember?"

He shook his head. But when Bailey raised an eyebrow, he nodded and paid the guy. He wrapped one hand up in the reins purely by reflex. The feel of the ropes in one hand and the saddle below him brought a surge of unexpected happiness. He raised a hand in the air, and the machine began.

Gracie jumped and clapped, and Bailey smiled. That smile brought him all the way back to a rodeo he'd done in high school. He'd been waiting in the box, sitting on the edge, ready to lower himself down on an angry bull. Then he'd met her eyes, waiting back behind the box for her barrel racing event, and her smile gave him everything he needed. All the fear left, and he'd won the event, setting a new record no one had yet beat to this day.

The mechanical bull beneath him jerked again, sudden and violent. Maverick was thrown to the ground.

He jumped up and started dusting himself off, but Bailey was already halfway to him, concern all over her face. "What happened? You okay?"

Chagrined, he could only shrug. "I guess you distracted me." It was the absolute truth.

"Mom won! Mom won!" Gracie jumped up and down and laughed.

Maverick nodded. "You are so right. This deserves an ice cream to celebrate. Who's in?"

Both girls raised their hands.

"Then we're off. I happen to know where to get the best ice cream in town."

As they crowded into a booth, he on one side and Bailey and Gracie on the other, he didn't think he could enjoy the moment any more than he already was. "Now, Gracie, I need to hear some stories about your mama, 'cause she's something special around here. And I'm betting she was something special wherever you guys were too."

Gracie nodded right away and scooped a spoonful of ice cream into her mouth. "She was, mm-hmm."

He waited.

"She's the best story reader I've ever heard." The girl nodded again, followed by another spoonful. "She reads me my top three and then even one more every night."

He was expecting something about her singing or playing guitars or something, but Gracie's reply was even better. "I can't think of anything more special. That's even better than winning the bull riding contest."

"Mm-hmm."

His gaze found Bailey's, and he reached for her hand across the table.

"What about you, Maverick?" Bailey asked. Then she turned to her daughter. "Did you know that Maverick here is a true rodeo star?"

"There was a time I might have been." He avoided her

face as he fiddled with his napkin, and she rushed to apologize.

"Of course. I'm sorry about your dad. Really sorry. This place isn't the same without him."

"Thank you. No, it's not." He shrugged it off. He wished it had been that easy when he'd turned down the first-place championship spot on the national rodeo team.

In many ways, it had been easy to know what he should do. He couldn't have told his mother that she would have to care for the ranch without him. But knowing what he should do and feeling happy about it were two different things. He still missed those days. He placed his napkin on the table. "There's something gripping about the words 'might have been.'"

Her gaze shot up to his, and he was struck by the power of what he'd just said. He was sitting sharing ice cream with the largest "might have been" of his life.

He shifted in his seat, releasing her hand. "So, what's a pretty pair of ladies like the two of you doing here without a handsome cowboy at your side?"

The grateful twinkle in Bailey's eyes told him she was ready for lighter topics. She raised one eyebrow. It wiggled for a moment like it always did when she was about to tease him. "Why, you know one?"

"I think I could wrangle one for you." He flexed.

And she laughed, but not before he saw a hint of appreciation as her gaze traveled over his arms and chest.

"'Cause me and the sweet pea, here, we're beginning to think that good cowboys are in short supply."

"They might be. We're a dying breed. But I could pull some strings."

Her grin widened, and her eyes were sincere. "Well, I

don't know if that will be necessary. I got the best one around right here." She looked away and then back. "If he still has time for that kind of thing."

"I've got time." He laughed. "Bailey, would you like to go to dinner with me?"

"Only if it involves—"

"Feed Store barbecue?"

"Exactly."

"I can arrange that. Tonight at seven?"

"Aren't we watching your brothers in their show tonight? And you?"

"Did they tell you that?" He shook his head. "They're always trying to rope me back in."

"We'd like to see you on a bull again." She turned to Gracie. "Wouldn't you like to see Uncle Maverick on a real bull?"

"Oh yes!" She clapped her hands again.

"Now that's just unfair." He sat back and crossed his arms. "I don't know how much longer I want to wait for our dinner. So how about this: I ride. Then you and I get drinks. And then we go out for dinner tomorrow."

Her cheeks colored, which he thoroughly enjoyed. "You're on."

For the next hour, they laughed and teased, and life was almost perfect. Then Maverick's alarm dinged. "Oh, that's my cue. Time to get backstage."

"You're really gonna do it?" The hope and sparkle in Bailey's face made him sit taller.

"I said I would, didn't I?"

"Yes, you did."

"And I am needed for other things, too."

"Oh, right, of course."

He stood and slid out of the booth. They did the same, and he very nearly leaned forward to kiss her, a quick peck just like old times. Before it became too obvious what he'd been about to do, he straightened and waved as he walked away.

She was as much a habit for him as she was new. But he couldn't be too embarrassed for his awkwardness. Everything around him seemed much more enjoyable. Even the prospect of getting on a bull again in front of his whole town. And it was all because Bailey was back. Could one person really have so much power over his happiness? He knew she could.

His heart clenched at the question that lingered whenever he thought of her. Was she here to stay?

Chapter 6

Bailey found two tickets waiting for her at the ticket booth for the closing-out show of the county fair. And the nostalgic pangs came back full force. The Dawson family tickets. She looked across the arena to a family of hands waving in her direction. She lifted Gracie so she could see, and the two waved back. She laughed and thought her heart might burst with happiness. Why had she ever thought this life confining? How could she have left?

They made their way around the stand, and she waved at a person here and there. They were good people. Not a single one had pressed her about why she'd left. They seemed ready to give her the space she needed. How had she been so blessed?

Then a jarring voice threw that sentiment out into the muck bin. "What on earth are you doing back here?"

"Tiff. Hey, how're you doing?"

"Just fine. We're all the same as we ever were. Picking up the pieces, comforting when necessary. This town has a good heart." She smirked and exchanged glances with the woman at her side, who Bailey didn't know.

"Well, great. Hey, I'm gonna go get our seats." Bailey hurried away, picking up Gracie so they could navigate the aisles faster.

"Who was that mean lady, Mom?" Gracie was so much more intuitive than Bailey would have thought any child could be.

"No one you need to be worrying about, that's for sure. She might not be so bad. She didn't say anything really mean, did she?" Her words sounded hollow. Tiff was probably as bad as ever. Bailey wondered—just like she undoubtedly wanted her to—if Tiff had run to comfort Maverick when Bailey left and how much Maverick had enjoyed the attention.

She shook her head. Bailey had no right to even entertain the thoughts running through her mind. Not after what she'd done, not after what felt like an even larger betrayal now that she was back home with everyone.

As they approached the family, the Dawsons scooted to make room for her and Gracie right in the middle of their group—right next to Maverick's mother. She sucked in her breath.

Under full scrutiny from one of the women she respected most in the world, she cowered. Mrs. Dawson's eyes stared into her face, making her feel as naked as their days skinny-dipping at the lake. She didn't deserve this woman's kindness nor her forgiveness.

Her eyes remained distant for a moment, calculating, but then she smiled, and her face filled with light. "Welcome home, child."

"Oh, Mrs. Dawson." She reached forward to wrap an

arm across her shoulders, but the woman pulled her into a full embrace.

"It's Mama to you, even still."

As she melted into the woman's strong softness, Bailey's worries slipped away for a moment.

"It's good to see you, honey."

When she finally pulled away, Bailey had to wipe away tears. Then she sucked in a breath before turning to her daughter. "And this is my daughter, Gracie. Honey, this is…" She turned, unsure. If Maverick was going to be an uncle…

Mrs. Dawson jumped in. "Call me Grandma Dawson."

"I have another grandma?" Gracie's eyes widened like she'd met a princess.

"Not a for-real grandma. But I don't have any grand-kids of my own yet, so I was wondering if I could practice on you for a while?"

Gracie's grin looked like it would break her face. "Yes, ma'am, I mean, Grandma."

Nash and Decker chuckled. And Nash winked. "She's a real charmer. Mama's gonna be smitten." He reached out for a fist bump. "Maybe it'll keep her happy enough she forgets we're the one barricade to her having heaps of her own grandkids."

"I hear you, Nash," his mom said. "And this is just going to make us all realize even more how important family is. Including marriage and all the blessings that come with it."

Nash sat back and shrugged.

Then the lights dimmed and flashed across the audi-ence. The announcer shouted into his microphone, "And now, we are pleased to present Willow Creek's one and only Maverick Dawson!"

The crowd went crazy, the strobe lights flashed, and confetti fell from the ceiling. And then Maverick stepped up to the microphone.

"Wow, what a welcome! Hello, Willow Creek!"

Everyone cheered. As Bailey's gaze traveled over the crowd and saw the families all together, the happiness in every corner, she hoped her daughter would finally have something good in her life.

"It's Friday night. You're at our hometown rodeo. It just doesn't get any better than this." Maverick's head turned, and she felt his gaze. This was the moment he used to salute her when he was riding, but this time, he just looked. She brought a hand up to her mouth and stopped herself from blowing a kiss, but just barely.

Then she watched as he honored good people in their town, talked up the 4-H program, and read announcements from the local church. Everyone loved him just like they had his father. Her heart swelled with pride. And a mean streak of insecurity.

She shrank into her seat, grateful that Gracie was playing around with Nash and Decker. Maverick deserved better than what she'd given him. She couldn't just show up in his life and hope that her messed-up pieces would mesh with their put-together pictures.

She thought she could do anything for Gracie, but as she looked at the amazing man in front of her, her parade of failures just about ground her down to the dust covering the arena floor.

How could she explain Daniel to anyone? How could she ever explain him to Maverick? The creep had offered her the world, all her dreams, fame, the ability to sing. She'd been naïve.

She shook her head. She'd tried to get past this. She'd left him, hadn't she? Sort of. She'd crawled away from him, a complete failure. No one had wanted to sign a deal with her. Daniel said he'd tried, but she just wasn't what they were looking for. And then he'd moved on. She started smelling perfume on him. She'd looked at herself in the mirror one morning after another night alone and told herself she'd gone as low as she was willing to go. She'd packed her bags and headed to a motel.

She squeezed her eyes tight against the tears that wanted to come.

Mrs. Dawson's soft hand reached around her shoulders and gave her a squeeze. "Now don't you worry. You're home now. Whatever it is, we can make it right."

Bailey shook her head, but she leaned into this strong woman who she'd always loved and whispered, "Thanks."

Then Maverick announced the first event: calf roping. "And to start us off, three-time rodeo champion with the second-place world record, doing a special presentation just for our audience tonight, let's hear it for Dylan Dawson!"

The crowd went crazy, and a group of women across the way screamed, "Dylan!" and held up a huge banner with his name on it.

Bailey laughed, and Mrs. Dawson clucked. "Oh, that's no way to win my Dylan."

Then the calf raced out into the arena with Dylan right behind him, spinning a lasso up above his head. It spun once, twice, then he threw it, caught the calf, jumped off his horse, wrapped the calf's legs, and stood.

"Wow, that's incredible!"

"He's gotten even faster. We think he might win that first-place record."

Bailey nodded.

Nash and Decker stood. "We need to go get set up backstage." Nash high-fived Gracie. "I'll see you later, princess."

Bailey smiled. Gracie wouldn't know what her real name was anymore with all the pet names she had acquired.

The clowns came out, and Gracie waved and squealed and jumped up and down. When they gave her a carnation, she thought her life was made. Then Maverick stepped back up to the microphone. "We will now announce the mutton bustin' contestants. As you know, seven lucky children from the audience will get to compete tonight, riding on the back of the sheep of their choice. The mutton buster who stays on longest wins a trophy and a new pair of Black Paw cowboy or cowgirl boots."

Everyone cheered, and Gracie asked, 'What's this?"

"It's fun! The kids get to ride a sheep."

"I wanna do it."

"Next time. We have to enter your name before the event."

Maverick read off the names: Tommy Rose, Julie Cadwell, Sally Jo Finway. Then he paused and looked right at Bailey. "Gracie Hempstead."

"What! Did he say my name, Mama?"

"Yes, he did, darling. That means you get to ride a sheep if you want to." Had Maverick added her name at the last minute?

"I want to!" She jumped up, and Bailey joined her.

"Could all the children please meet down by the mutton bustin' chutes near the Black Paw Boots sign."

Gracie skipped forward, pulling on her hand, and Bailey had to follow her. When they arrived at the sign, the arena staff gave each child a helmet and vest and then went over how things were going to go. Bailey hardly heard a word. Gracie jumped up and down with excitement until the first child was lowered down into a tall wooden slip and onto the back of a sheep.

Gracie's worried voice tugged at Bailey's awareness. "I don't want to, Mommy."

"Oh, what? Well, honey, that's okay."

Maverick approached. "What did I hear? Is our Gracie about to be a star?"

"A star?"

"Sure! Did you know that all the contestants are gonna be on TV today?"

"Really? Like, will Grandma see me?"

"She sure will. Come here, let me show you how this works. I've got some tips on how to win this thing." He winked at Bailey and brought her daughter over to the chute. They peeked down while the second contestant was lowered onto the next sheep.

As Bailey watched, her love for Maverick grew. The familiarity and love from her younger years expanded. Such a good man did not deserve someone like her, and he sure didn't deserve what she'd done to him. Why hadn't younger Bailey seen what was so obvious to her now?

On the day of their wedding, she had stared and stared at his picture in her bridal room. She willed him to be enough, prayed he'd be enough, wished, cried, and hoped she could find satisfaction in this life, in a small-town home with Maverick. But something inside had turned away and grabbed the selfish path, had reached for her dream. Wasn't that what people said to do? Go after your dream, or you'll regret it for the rest of your life.

So she had, and what did she regret? She looked down. She regretted ever leaving in the first place. But as she watched her daughter, she realized she couldn't regret everything.

And then it was time for Gracie to sit on the sheep. When Gracie shook her head no, Bailey was about to rescue her from Maverick's encouragement, but he held up a finger, so she waited. And then a moment later, Gracie nodded, gave Maverick a fist bump, and allowed the staff to lower her down onto the back of a sheep.

Bailey ran forward. "You got this, honey. You can do this. Just listen to Uncle Maverick."

Her little girl grabbed onto the sheep's fleece, closed her eyes, and buried her head into the side of the animal.

Bailey's fists clenched as the gate opened and the sheep tore out into the arena. The announcer called out, "Gracie Hempstead on the back of sheep number five."

Huge cheers tore out from the Dawson brothers backstage, and Bailey watched the clock. "What does she have to beat?"

"Six seconds."

"That's it?"

"It's harder than it looks. But she's a rock star. And the youngest one out there."

Her sheep tore out across to the far end of the arena. It kicked up its back legs, and Bailey thought for sure Gracie would be thrown, but she clung on.

"Yes!" Maverick cheered under his breath.

The clock counted, four, five, six…

The sheep tore back toward them, racing faster and faster.

Seven, eight… The crowd erupted in cheers. Nine. Ten.

Her sheep stopped abruptly, and Gracie toppled to the ground. The clowns ran forward and dusted her off. Over the loudspeaker, they all heard, "Gracie Hempstead, from right here in Willow Creek, is the winner and this year's new record holder with an amazing score of ten seconds. Congratulations, Gracie Hempstead!"

They led her back, and as she walked out of the arena, she turned and waved to Grandma Dawson. Then she picked up her feet and came tearing through the gate and up into Bailey's arms. "I did it! I did it!"

"You sure did, honey. I'm so proud of you."

"I am too." Maverick rested a hand on her back. "Did you hear? You're a county champ now."

"I am?"

"You sure are. You get to stand on the podium next to Uncle Dylan and receive your trophy."

Her eyes widened. "Wow."

They laughed. And Bailey said, "Thank you. She'll never forget this."

"Oh, there's more to come. She's a natural. We're gonna get her riding horses. Maybe she can be a barrel racer like her mom." He paused. "Anyway, it was special to get to help her like that. Thanks." He nodded his head and turned away.

She knew he was busy—he had another event to announce—but she also knew he was running away because things had gotten too personal. And she couldn't blame him. She was a mess, and he deserved better.

Chapter 7

Maverick was a mess. He was finally ready to admit it. Every new event he announced, he kept looking at his girl in the stands just like he used to. Only she wasn't his girl. What even were they? She hadn't explained why she left, and he didn't know how long she was staying.

Why did he ask her out? To torture himself. If his brothers could hear his thoughts, they'd send him away on a horse to figure himself out. He laughed. That's what his dad used to do to them. Any time they were not acting like themselves, they were sent off on a horse to figure it out. Looking back, he saw the wisdom in that. He wondered if he'd ever be half the man his father was.

He wondered if he'd ever get to be a father. For many years, he'd almost given up on the idea. But now…

He shook his head.

Nash and Decker and Dylan approached. Nash had just wasted the world record for bronc riding, and Decker had thoroughly entertained everyone on the back of a bull.

"You're going in tonight," Decker said.

Maverick bristled. He'd already been thinking about it, and he'd promised Gracie. So why was Decker coming at him like this? "Oh yeah?"

Nash faced him on Decker's other side. "Yeah. It's time you got off your duff and took the reins on the sort of life you actually want."

Fire bubbled up from out of nowhere. "Because it's so easy to just selfishly do whatever I want."

"You saying I'm selfish?" Nash bristled.

"I'm not saying anything. If you went there, you should take a look in the mirror."

Decker stepped closer. "Hey, now. Whoa. This was meant to be funny. We have an idea to get Bailey out there, too."

Maverick listened—the idea had merit. He nodded. "We'll do it next time. Tonight's not the night for that kind of stuff."

Nash was about to argue, but Maverick cut him off. "I said I'd do it. If you want Bailey involved, though, you need to give her some time."

They high-fived each other, and as his brothers walked away, Nash's voice carried back to him. "Maverick Dawson, back in the saddle."

He sure liked the sound of that. He liked being on the rodeo floor. That's why he agreed to emcee the county rodeos as often as he did. He loved the energy. He loved the whole show, and if he could be a part of it, he was not gonna turn down the opportunity. But ride a bull? Gracie's wide eyes looking up at him floated back across his mind's eye. He'd told the little girl he would ride. So he was gonna ride.

He made his way down a long hall and into the costume shop. Somewhere in here was his old gear.

"What can I get for you, darling?" Nellie sat at a table, mending clothing. She'd been here as long as he could remember. She's what kept them looking good.

"I'm looking for my old gear. Or any costume, something to wear out there."

She jumped up out of her seat and rushed to the back. Then she returned, carrying the costume he'd worn during his last two rodeo circuits.

"Wow, it still looks like new."

"I've been taking care of it for you."

"Someone else could have worn it. I donated it."

"And here you are, needing it again. You just trust that Nellie knows her stuff." She pushed the glasses up on her nose. "Besides, no one would ever wear your gear. It's yours, same as that record of yours no one can touch."

He chuckled. "Well, thank you. I appreciate you taking care of this for me."

She nodded and went back to work, but her small smile told him how happy she was. She was a dear old lady, an icon of the rodeo.

He slipped into a dressing room. He used to have one with his name on it. The dim lighting, the wall full of mirrors, the smell. He closed his eyes. Horses, manure, popcorn, and barbecue. What a mixture.

As soon as he had himself all spiffed up, he took a moment to review his mental game before getting on the bull. Be lithe, be soft, grip the straps, move with the animal. Know when to let go.

He stepped out of the dressing room feeling more alive

than he had in a long time. Since the day of his almost wedding.

Nellie whistled at him as he walked by her.

He rested his fingers on her table. "I'll have these back and washed."

"Keep 'em. I have a feeling you're gonna be needing them."

He didn't try to contradict her, and he wished she were right. His days on the circuit had been some of his happiest. Even though it made finishing college difficult, even though it took him away from Bailey, he had fit in everything that was important and was still able to compete. He exited the long back hall, and immediately people took note. Phones came out, and kids called out to him.

"You gonna ride, Maverick?" the man behind the hot dog concessions called to him.

"I sure am."

"Folks, I'm closing up shop early," the man announced. "If Maverick's gonna ride, I gotta get out there to see it."

Maverick smiled. It sure felt good to be remembered.

Then he made his way to the bull pens. He quieted his mind so he could focus.

The announcer came on to call for the last barrel racer. He announced all the upcoming rodeos that would be passing through Willow Creek. And then he paused.

"Now, folks, I have a special announcement for you. For the first time in over five years, our very own, professional, world champion..."

As soon as he said those words, the crowd erupted, and Maverick laughed. He loved this. Was that wrong? How could it be? Those stands were full of the people he loved, people he worked with side by side, people he went to church with, and here they were, happy that he would ride.

He climbed up on the fencing surrounding Pepper, the bull he would be riding tonight. His hands were wrapped. Then he bowed his head. Before every ride, he asked for protection. When he opened his eyes, a familiar peace had settled over. He was ready.

He lowered himself on the back of the massive animal and was lost to the moment. The crowd quieted. The huge arena went still. And he and the animal waited. He could feel the powerful gulps of air as the bull shifted beneath his thighs. He measured his breaths.

Then he nodded; the door opened, and he and the bull burst from the chute. The animal kicked, rolled, twisted, and jerked under him, and his body moved with him. Seconds passed. Everything moved slower. His bull was going crazy, as if he wanted Maverick with a vengeance. Good. The worse the bull behaved, the more points Maverick could receive. He kept his body pliable, looking for a rhythm. It had been so long, his body hungered for the abuse. At last, eight long seconds later, the horn blew, and he hopped off Pepper. But the bull was not done with him yet. In an uncharacteristic move, he turned on Maverick with his horns lowered.

He jumped up on the railing while the bull fighters ran out to distract the angry bull. Pepper rammed his horns into the wood just below where Maverick had been. The animal ran around and around the arena, still kicking and bucking until he finally calmed somewhat, and with a couple whips cracking, he returned to his chute.

Maverick whooped and swung his hat around in the air. That ride would have won him some serious points if he were in competition, probably a full fifty points for difficulty of the bull. He wiped his forehead. But he'd forgotten just how much a hard ride like that racked his body. He gently rolled his head, stretching out his neck.

Nash ran up. "You just had a near-perfect ride."

"I don't know——"

"No, I had a rodeo judge standing next to me, and he said that ride would have blown your old record out of the water. Near perfect."

Maverick considered him. Points like that in another competition would be career shaping. Would give him a name and a face on the circuit for the rest of his lifetime. "Wow, man. I haven't even ridden in years."

"It's still in you. You should do this!"

Maverick shook his head. "And ask you to sit out the circuit this year so I can go in your place?"

Nash's face clouded, and he looked away.

"Someone's gotta keep the ranch together. If I leave, someone else has to stay." And that's where the conversation stopped. Just like Maverick knew it would.

Maverick's ride was the last event of the evening. The announcer ended the show, and people started heading down the stairs and out the doors.

Just about everyone wanted a piece of Maverick, to congratulate him, to talk strategy, to tell him how much they'd love it if he rode again. But all he wanted was to escape with Bailey. He searched over the heads of the crowd and didn't see her for the longest time.

At last, when the crowd had thinned, he spotted her leaning up against the wall. She waved to him.

He shook one more hand and took two steps toward her, then a pair of arms flew around his middle, squeezing tight. "Maverick! That was incredible! I was so proud of you, babe!" Tiff lifted up on her toes to tell him something, but he couldn't hear, so he leaned down, and she kissed his cheek.

His gaze flew to Bailey. She had started to move toward him, but she stopped, hesitation written all over her. Then she pivoted and walked in the opposite direction.

Tiff wrapped her hands around his arm and began pulling him toward the exit. "We're meeting at Buck's, come with us." She pressed her body against his arm.

He pulled his hand out of her grip, but she stepped into him and pressed her cheek to his chest. "It's been too long. Let's just go somewhere and relax. Let me rub you down, work out those kinks."

He shook his head and tried to step away, but her grip was insistent.

All he wanted was to talk to Bailey. But while trying to peel himself away from Tiff, his gaze caught Bailey's. She shook her head and kept walking.

"Tiff, stop. I already have plans tonight."

Her lower lip went out, and she placed a hand on her hip. "I'm just trying to help you get out, be young, enjoy your friends."

"Thank you, really. You and your mama have been kind." He had to get to Bailey before she left.

"Of course, babe. I'm here for you. You know that." She took a half-step toward him again, but he stepped back and then began to move away.

"I'll see you around?" Without waiting for an answer, he took off running across the parking lot. At first, he didn't see Bailey anywhere. But as he spun around, his gaze was drawn by a lone figure, walking.

He took off after her. She was as stubborn as ever. He'd always had to work for her affection. She had zero tolerance for the women after shows, even girls wanting selfies. It looked like things hadn't changed. Whether or not she had a right to be, Bailey was proprietary where he was concerned. He'd always liked that about her. He'd had no problems being true to her. She'd been worth it—until she left.

The thought triggered a rush of irritation, and he stopped running. *Why am I chasing after a woman who can't wait around for thirty minutes while I talk to people?* He whistled.

Bailey kept right on walking.

Chapter 8

Bailey walked home. They lived about two miles from the county fairgrounds. It was far, but she couldn't stomach anyone's company. Especially not Maverick's.

Did she have any right to expect that he'd be single? No. Did she have any right to be annoyed that Tiff had her hands all over him? No. But Bailey was more than annoyed. She was spitting angry and knew she had to leave before she laid into Maverick like they were still in high school.

He was probably standing in the parking lot, fuming mad at her, too. She kicked her boots against the pavement. At least Gracie'd had a ride home. No need for her to see her mama like this.

Once she'd pounded the full two miles back to her house, she felt much better and a little sheepish. She wanted to get drinks with Maverick. But she didn't know how to get ahold of him. He'd probably already gone out with the gang, taken Tiff up on her offer.

She climbed the porch stairs and nearly jumped out of

her skin when her dad said, "Maverick still being a gentleman?"

She swallowed twice and caught her breath. "Oh. Ha. Yes, Daddy. He's the best kind of gentleman."

"Then why is my baby girl walking her own self home?"

"Oh, you know me. I had to get something out of my system."

"Come sit by your old man."

She laughed. "You're not old." But really, he was getting up there, and the thought made her throat clench.

"So, what did he do?"

She shook her head. "Oh, Daddy, honestly, it's more what I did. I messed up, and I don't know how to make it all right...again." The despairing thought that her whole life could be summed up as a list of mistakes she didn't know how to fix only made her feel worse.

He patted her shoulder. "We all do that sometimes in our life, I reckon. Do you know a single person who hasn't messed up pretty bad?"

She snorted. "Yeah. No one here has ever messed up as bad as I have."

"Oh, I'm sure they have. Just no one's anxious to talk about it, are they?"

"Mm."

"Yours just happens to be more public than most."

"Yeah, I wish so bad I could turn back time."

"Don't we all. But where would you be then? What would your heart be telling you?"

She thought about it and admitted, "To run off. My dumb, selfish heart would be calling out for the chance to make it big, telling me all of this wasn't good enough." She shook her head.

"Now, that's not such a bad thing for a heart to say. You love singing. You always have."

She wasn't gonna let her father help her feel better about running away.

"I'm not telling you that you went about it the right way. You about near broke your mama's heart."

She sucked in a breath. And then nodded.

"And now this ain't easy, realizing we missed out on five years of our precious granddaughter's life."

Bailey shrank in her chair.

"But you're here now. And what can we do but focus on that?"

"I was sick, Daddy. I was desperate. I wanted to be someone. I guess it took me hitting rock bottom to realize that was never gonna happen."

"And that's the whole beauty of what happened."

"Me hitting rock bottom?"

"Yep. I don't like hearing any news of you being sad, but look where you are. You're not the same person who left, are you?"

"How can I know that?"

"Well, if you were in the same situation again now. If you were about to marry Maverick and somebody called with your next big break, what would you do?"

She shook her head. "I'd never go. I wouldn't." She smiled. "You're right." That felt amazing.

"Now see. Just like I told you. You've learned. And that's the whole point. That's why God lets us do some of the things we do. And then when we come back to Him, he helps us make it right. His Grace is everything. He already bore all these burdens you're carrying around inside. He's felt them and he's taken them on so you don't have to." He put his arm around her. "Besides that, I don't see why you have to give up your singing, darling."

"No." She shook her head. "Don't say that. It's a powerful dream, and I don't want anything to do with it anymore. It stole everything from me: my happiness, the only man I'll ever love, my parents. That curse of a dream sucked me into its promises and lies. Daniel…" She looked away. She'd never spoken her ex-boyfriend's name to her parents. "He led me along like a crazed puppet believing his lies."

"And you were trapped."

"In a way, yes."

They sat for a while, both lost in thought. Her thoughts were full of regret. For her weak choices, for her five years away. And almost as powerfully, this time for not turning around to go get drinks with Maverick.

"You could still go out with him tonight."

She shook her head. "Nah. He's probably long gone, out with friends."

"Nope." Her dad chuckled. "I happen to know that's not true."

"What?" She searched her dad's face and then looked around their front yard. "Is he here?"

Maverick stepped out from the shadow of the trees to the left of the house.

She crossed her arms and narrowed her eyes. "You been listening to me?"

He shook his head. "Nope."

"Why you here?"

"Be nice to him, Bailey," her dad murmured.

"I'm trying. He just makes me crazy."

"That ain't so bad."

She considered her dad, his eyes twinkling, and her smile lifted in a grin. "No, it ain't." She stood, took a half-step toward Maverick, and then paused.

———

MAVERICK HAD ONLY STAYED mad for about five minutes, then he'd followed her home to make sure she got there okay. Was he a sorry sap of a man? When it came to Bailey, yes, he guessed he was.

She turned to say something to her dad. So he called out before she could change her mind. "Come with me."

Her shoulders dropped, and then she turned back to him. "You still wanna go out?" Her insecurity, the despairing expression on her face, tore at him. This was not the Bailey he knew. She looked like the colt who had been trained by an overly harsh breaker: submissive, yes, but out of fire.

"Oh, hey, come here, you." He held out his arms and stepped closer. She jumped down the stairs, and when he was close enough, she melted into his arms. "Of course, I still want to spend time with you. And tomorrow, too, if you think my big head can fit through the door."

She laughed and looked up into his face. "You're an idiot. I don't think you'd get a truly big head no matter what happened to you. You're already the best in the world, and tonight probably beat your old record. If that hasn't ruined you, nothing can."

"Not likely to, anyway. It felt good, though, all those people calling my name. Maverick! Maverick!" He whispered a crowd-like noise and then bumped her shoulder. "I wanna see you out there again. It felt great, Bailey! Even just one time."

For a moment, her eyes lit with interest, but then she went solemn again. "Maybe I'll get to do barrel racing again. But, Maverick, we've gotta talk. I have some things I need to tell you, and I just realized I can't be putting it off any longer."

Maverick's hope flared. Would he finally get some answers? "Do you just want to go back to my truck? We can talk inside."

She shrugged.

"Come on. It can't be as bad as all that."

But the look she gave him made him wonder.

They made their way back to the truck and hopped inside. He pulled out his flannel blanket from behind the seat and handed her a thermos. "Hot chocolate."

"Of course, you brought the hot cocoa."

He turned the truck on for a moment to get the heat going, and then he twisted in his seat so that he was facing her. "You know, having you back is doing crazy things with my emotions."

Her eyes widened. "Mine too."

"Like this right here. How many times have we sat across from each other in this truck? I see you over there, an adult, a mother, but my mind remembers us as teenagers, as college kids, engaged..."

Her face pinched in pain, but he couldn't spare her the truth. If he was ever going to understand what happened, to have some closure, he would need answers. And frankly, he deserved them.

"I don't know where to start." Her gaze flitted to his

and then away, but he just waited. Finally, she cleared her throat and hugged herself. "I know nothing I say will make it right. So I hope you're not over there thinking I have some magical reason for being a terrible person. Understanding won't make it easier not to hate me." She shook her head. "I know that nothing I could say is good enough. There would never be a good enough reason for what I did to you, to my parents, to Gracie." She choked on her daughter's name and looked away. "But you deserve to know that I loved you. I wanted to spend the rest of my life with you and forever after. I didn't leave because I wanted to run away from *you*."

He nodded, not quite sure he believed her. But he hoped what she said was true.

"I don't know, Maverick. Here's what I think happened. I looked at our lives, looked at you and all that you had going for you. Rodeo star, circuit after circuit. You were the world champion that year, remember? I couldn't take that away from you."

"What are you talking about? Why would you—"

"I'll explain, Maverick. I wasn't happy."

He tried to ignore his pain at those words. He'd worried for years that he hadn't been enough for her, that he hadn't made her happy.

"Everything with you was perfect, but I wanted more. I was selfish. I wanted a career of my own, in music. I wanted people shouting *my* name. You had a world record. I wanted a piece of that too."

"What do you mean? Like, as a singer?"

"Yes, I know that sounds ridiculous."

He opened his mouth, but she talked over him.

"Especially now that I know what an epic failure I was.

But at the time, I looked around at this beautiful town, at all these lovely people, my family, your family, and I wanted more.

"I was gonna ask you if we could take off for a year and live in Nashville so I could see where this went. But then you got your record and signed that deal to ride the circuit for two more years."

He nodded. "I should have talked to you first."

"You did. We talked about it, remember? Right here in this truck. And when you showed me the contract, when you had that light in your eyes and I knew I was witnessing your dream coming true, I couldn't say anything but 'go for it.'"

He should have pushed, asked her questions. He'd been so completely dizzy with excitement at his new fame he hadn't bothered to really make sure she was on board.

"And then someone called me. A man named Daniel. He said he'd represent me, help me make it big, introduce me to producers. But I had to go to Nashville right then. There was a group of producers looking for a new talent. And Daniel said if we didn't leave soon, I would miss my window."

"So you went."

"I went. He offered me a room at his place, and I never left."

"And Gracie?"

"He's her father."

Maverick nodded. He didn't know what to say. If he said what he was actually thinking, he might never be able to take it back. "Did you love him?

"That's not a fair question."

"Why not? Seems fair to me. Did you or didn't you?"

She shook her head. "No. But…he told me he'd get me a contract. He told he we'd take the world and I'd be a star…" She looked away. He could see she was in pain, but he didn't want to comfort her, not yet.

She continued, "But I was a coward. I couldn't tell you. I couldn't break your heart and see it with my own eyes."

"So you ran and never looked back?"

She shook her head, the tears falling freely now, wetting her cheeks. "I looked back, every single day. I looked back the very next morning, but I saw the papers, I saw people's posts. Everyone was so mad at me. I knew I'd broken your heart. I couldn't face it."

She looked out the window, her pain obvious in the lines of her face. "I know what you're thinking. But I warned you. Nothing I say is meant to make you feel better."

"Then, what?"

"Well, then I learned he'd lied. There was no team of producers ready to hear my talent. He had no connections. He was as young and green as I was. We tried to get as many auditions as we could. I sang anywhere that had a gig —bars, lots of bars, people's parties, private events." She looked away with such an expression of guilt he wondered what burdens she was carrying.

"Look, Bailey, I'm not saying what you did was okay or anything, but it's done, right? If you had to sing at a few gigs that made you uncomfortable, you learned that it wasn't your thing."

She didn't answer. But he could tell she was considering what he said. Then she took a shuddering breath. "So one day, I smelled perfume on Daniel's shirt. And saw the lipstick. It all sounds so cliché, but she was the new potential, the talent, the possible star, and I was a failure. He kicked me out when he found out I was pregnant."

"What?" Maverick's temper flared, but he kept it under wraps. What kind of lazy lowlife backed away from his responsibility like that?

Then he considered what Bailey'd been through. "Where did you go? What did you do?"

"It just gets more and more cliché. I waitressed. I sang small gigs. I worked at the local department store, trying to make a name for myself, trying desperately to prove I was not a failure."

He opened his mouth.

"And don't say it. I know I should have come home, but you don't understand. You will never understand what it feels like to fail. To let everyone you know down in such an unforgivably epic way and then try to live every day to make up for that fact. It's a living hell, and I was stuck in it."

He reached for her hand, but she waved him away. "What if I'd come home? What then? I run to Nashville, get pregnant, and then come running back so y'all can pick up the pieces for me? No, I was gonna fix it first. Make a life for myself, and then come home." She shook her head. "So I did that. Lived that life, trying so hard to be something, anything, other than a failure. Until I just couldn't anymore. We were living on welfare. Rent was way too high. I couldn't even get Gracie started in school. We lived in my car. Maverick. My car. So I came home. I came back for my daughter. I knew even if I failed at parenting, my parents were pretty dang great, and they could give Gracie the life she deserves."

So she hadn't come home for him. But she'd been through way more than he'd imagined.

"Maverick, I'm sorry. You deserve better. So much better. I wish you were really, truly happy right now so I didn't know deep inside that I'd ruined everything for you as well as for me."

He leaned back in his seat and faced the windshield.

"Being back here means I failed. It means I'm nothing. I messed up so bad not even I can fix it, and I'm just hoping my parents can pick up the pieces and make something special for Gracie."

He closed his eyes. He knew he needed to say something to Bailey. His heart broke all over again for her. And for his own failures. "I'm sorry. Bailey, I'm sorry I wasn't there for you, sorry I didn't listen or consider that my plans might not be your plans. I messed up."

"No, Maverick, that's not what happened. You deserve better—"

"I know I do."

"Oh." She seemed to shrink.

"Look. I've got some things to deal with here. This is a lot. I'll be honest. But there's one thing you gotta do."

"What's that?"

"You have got to let God do His part. You're talking like this is all on you. Yes, you did some selfish things. You broke Hearts. But He knew we'd all do dumb things. He paid a price for a reason." It hurt him to say any of these things when he was hurting right then, when everything she told him was causing him pain.

She opened her mouth and then closed it, with a small shake of her head.

"I'm sorry you went through what you did. But I gotta

let this settle for a few days. What you said…you're right. None of this makes it any better. I got so many things to think about now, I don't know where to begin."

"I understand."

But she couldn't understand. She had no way of knowing that he was gonna sit up all night wondering what would have happened if he'd known what Bailey was going through. He was gonna replay all the moments he should have encouraged her to chase her dream. She'd wanted her own success. Why hadn't he seen that at the time? Why hadn't she just told him? He was gonna relive that hour he'd waited at the head of the church with everyone in town looking at him. At first, the looks had been amused, then sympathetic, and then outright pitying.

He'd think about his dad dying and how she hadn't been there, how he'd had to ignore his grief and push forward for the family. He was gonna wish she hadn't been with another man. Wish that Gracie was actually his child, their daughter. He was gonna go through all the garbage that these last five years had brought him, and then he was gonna let it go. He'd pray for help and then throw it away.

He had to.

Chapter 9

Days had gone by. A full week. Bailey tried to move forward with the same hope she'd felt when she arrived at her parents' house. But Maverick hadn't reached out since their talk, and she found it hard to think about anything else. The hurt in his face had nearly destroyed her. And then his final words to her…she closed her eyes. "Let God do His part." She shook her head. Did God have a part in her life even after all she'd done?

Bailey waited in her car, waited for the courage to go to something so simple as a job interview. A position opened up at the middle school, so she called and set up an interview for this morning. And now she had to get out of the car, walk across the parking lot, enter the school building, and try to convince them she'd make a good teacher. She was early, so she had some time, but she couldn't make herself get out of her car. She sat, staring at her steering wheel.

They were looking for a choir director, and Bailey would love to take that job. She could sing, help her students develop their talents, choose their music, maybe even write songs for them. But how could she present herself in a way that would make them want to hire her? She was a mess. She was unreliable. She'd failed at everything she'd tried and had no references or anyone who could vouch for her.

The entire town knew what she'd done to Maverick. That alone negated most job skills that would be of value. She didn't really think they would hire her, but when they asked her for an interview, she'd been hopeful.

Her phone beeped; a video call was coming in. Gracie's face filled her screen. "Hi, Mommy."

"Hey there, sugarplum. How's it going?" Just seeing her daughter's face ignited a spark of hope inside of her.

"I'm good. Grandpa said I can ride the pony today."

"You're gonna love it. Isn't Grandpa good?"

"Yeah." Her small pout came out.

"What's wrong, honey?"

"He's good, but I miss you. Nobody's as good as you, Mom."

Her throat tightened, and her eyes welled up. "Thank you, Gracie."

She made a heart with her two hands, and Bailey rested the phone on her dash so she could do the same. "Now, I gotta go in there and get us a job. What do you think I should tell them so they'll hire me?"

"Tell them you're just what they need."

"I like that. I think you're absolutely right. And, Gracie?"

"Yeah."

"You're just what I need." She kissed the screen and hung up.

For a moment, Bailey thought that maybe she *was* good enough, and she was thankful all over again for such a precious daughter. Gracie deserved so much more than Bailey had given her.

Filled with a new determination, she opened the door, straightened her back, stood as tall as she could, and walked with purpose through the front door of the middle school.

They offered her the job on the spot. She smiled. The goodness of the people of this town was evident all around her. Someone had called ahead to recommend her. They wouldn't say who, but whoever it was had cleared an easy path for her to be hired.

They'd heard about her at the rodeo, knew she could sing, and with her degree, she was a good candidate, anyway. Now, as she drove back to her parents' house, she could only smile. Perhaps she could make a life for herself after all. As she walked out the door, she whispered, "Thank you God." It was a start.

Her phone dinged. When she stopped at a traffic light, she glanced down. Alarm flitted through her. *Daniel*. She pulled over to the side of the road and, with shaking hands, opened her texts.

Hey, babe. I saw your daughter on television last night. Did she win a rodeo event? That's incredible. Call me. I'd love to hear about her.

No. Oh no, no, no. Bailey's first reaction was to block his number. He could not weasel his way into their lives. He didn't deserve to be there. But then she closed her eyes and breathed four times, trying to calm her beating heart. He *was* Gracie's father. And she deserved to have her father in her life. It would be good for her. Wasn't that what all the studies said? Could she deny her child a father who was showing signs that he wanted to be a part of her life?

Could she actually welcome him in, though? She shook her head. She didn't think so. That man had ruined her life. No, she'd ruined her own life, throwing away everything that was good, everything she loved for his false promises. He'd used her and then thrown her out.

Of all the things she'd done for Gracie—coming home, facing her town, facing Maverick—she couldn't be expected to do one more hard thing. Could she? Was she supposed to involve Daniel in their lives?

She thought about Maverick and his brothers. They were a product of their awesome dad. But look at Maverick now, left in the world without his father. Would he have been the man he'd become if he'd been raised only by his mother? She had no way of knowing.

But Mr. Dawson had been awesome. He *was* the Dawson name. Everyone in town had loved him. If he'd run for mayor, he would have won. Whatever he did, he worked hard until he succeeded. He was honor personified. But Daniel... She cringed. Daniel was a weasel. What kind of man would Maverick have become if raised by a weasel?

Who could she talk to about this? Now more than ever, she craved advice. Could she talk to her parents about this sort of thing? She didn't want to involve them in the emotional turmoil in her life. Bearing it on her own was hard enough; did those she loved really deserve to have to endure everything along with her?

She just didn't know what to do.

Her phone dinged again. With a feeling of dread, she lifted it to see the text.

Maverick. Just seeing his name eased the tightness that was building in her chest.

Hey, I'd love to see you. Let's start there.

Could she confide in Maverick?

She texted back, *Okay.*

How about right now?

Lol. Sounds good. I'm halfway between the school and home. Meet me at Sam's?

Be there in five.

Sam's was their high school hangout with the best burger she'd ever eaten and a special fry sauce that rivaled any she'd ever tasted. The owner, Judy, said it was her own special recipe, and whatever it was, it made Bailey smile every time it passed her lips.

She pulled into the parking lot. Maverick's truck was already out front. Instead of fighting the teenage thrill that jolted her heart into gear, she accepted it. Maverick was her man. He always had been. Did that mean anything for their future? Maybe. Or maybe not. It didn't matter. She was just gonna accept that, no matter what he wanted, she was his.

They made their way into Sam's. At the familiar ding when they pushed the door open, Bailey smiled and breathed in the memories that swirled in the air with the delicious aromas. Judy came around from the back, wiping her hands on her apron. "Is that Bailey I see?" Her eyes twinkled with such warmth that Bailey ran forward.

"Oh, Judy." She flung her arms around the woman like she was family. "I'm so happy to see you."

She stiffened a little, so Bailey stepped away. "Oh, me too, dear. Now, you just make yourself comfortable. I'll be out in a sec to bring you whatever you want. Anything—on the menu or not." She leaned closer and whispered, "Mav-

erick's waiting. But, honey, remember you be good to him."
Her eyes were kind, but Bailey could see maybe Judy's heart
had been hurt when Bailey left too.

Bailey nodded. "Thanks." Then she lifted her gaze to
meet Maverick's. He sat in the corner booth, his arm over
the back, his hat tipped up so she could get a good look at
his face. His plaid work shirt was stretched across his broad
shoulders and chest. Maverick the man was so much more
than Maverick the youth. She imagined he turned every
woman's head, not just her own.

"Thanks," she murmured again, not seeing anything
else but Maverick. His eyes were trained on her as she
stepped toward the back of the diner. She couldn't look
away. Did she sit next to him in the crook of his arm like
she always had, or did she sit across from him?

He winked and indicated she sit right where she
always had.

She laughed and sat as close as she dared. Could this be
happening? Was she free to forget her troubles for a minute
and pretend she and Maverick were back together?

"I'm so happy we can be friends again, Bailey."

Friends. Much of her euphoria fizzled out with that one
word. What more did she deserve, really? He couldn't be
expected to even trust her after what she did.

"Me too." She smiled.

Judy approached. "Now, this is a sight I wasn't sure I'd
ever see again." She smiled at them. Her eyes held warning,
but she said, "I'm so happy you two are together again."

Bailey sucked in her breath. "We're—"

"—happy too," Maverick finished for her.

What was he doing?

Judy pulled a pencil out from behind her ear. "What are

84

we having tonight?" She pointed at Bailey. "If you were eighteen, I'd say you're the regular burger without onions, fries and sauce, and a strawberry shake."

Bailey grinned. "That's the best meal you serve. I'd like exactly that."

Maverick shook his head. "Ho, ho, not the best meal, the second best. I'd like your barbecue double with cheese, and I agree on the fries and sauce. *That's* your best meal."

"Done. And to drink?"

"Chocolate shake for old times."

When she turned away, Bailey shook her head. "She's something. I missed her almost as much as my own mom."

"I think she can take credit for helping to raise half the kids in this town."

"She really can. I remember she sat me down one time to talk about girl stuff and how to handle the mean girls in middle school." She sipped the water Judy had left them. Bailey expected Judy's version of the inquisition would come sooner or later. And after all the times they'd talked, she deserved her own explanation.

Maverick leaned closer. "Thanks for explaining things the other night, Bailey. The hardest part was not knowing." The pain in his voice and on his face brought immediate tears to her eyes.

"I'm sorry, Maverick. You didn't deserve it. Would it help to talk about it?"

He fiddled with his napkin. "I think so. At any rate, there are a few things I'd like you to know. And this will be quick. I want today to be fun and relaxed, the start of something new." He frowned. "But I have to say a few things. You should have called, texted, sent a message through a friend, anything. We all care about you. We were worried. We didn't know if you'd been hurt, or abducted, or what. Not until the first paper picked you up."

Bailey dipped her head. "You're so right. I'll try to make it up to everyone somehow. I was scared. It was hard to own up to doing something so terrible. And I didn't want everyone trying to convince me to come back. So I ghosted."

He didn't answer.

"And I know that doesn't make it okay."

"The other thing I want you to know is that all these years, all this time, I've loved you. You're the only woman I've ever loved. You were my first and only girlfriend. You're the one, Bailey."

Her heart tripped in hope.

"But I'm in a strange position. My heart might be shouting for you, but my brain is telling me to stop. I just don't know enough to know where this should go." He searched her face. "And I can't tell where you see this going either." He fiddled with his napkin. "So, as long as you know I'm a mess, we're good."

"I came here with no expectations. I'm the one with nothing to offer. You owe me nothing, that's for sure."

He nodded. "You're a part of my life, my family's life, no matter what. Can we do friends?"

"I'd feel really lucky, actually."

Judy brought their food. "Here you go, sweethearts. When Cook heard it was you, he added some extras." She smiled and left them to themselves.

Bailey stole one of his fries.

"Hey!"

"Yours always taste better." She dipped it in her strawberry shake. "Mmm. At last." She closed her eyes. "These really are the best fries no matter where you go."

"Glad to hear I'm not missing out on some secret, amazing fries in Nashville."

"No way. Judy has something special here."

They ate for a few minutes with Bailey loving every bite. *Friends.* She would love to be back in Maverick's life. Seeing his mom, his brothers, made her realize all the more how much she was missing out on when she wasn't a part of the Dawson clan.

"So tell me about your interview. Did they offer you the position?"

"They did! On the spot."

"That's awesome. They're lucky to have you."

"I hope so. I was super happy. It's like something's finally going right again." She bit her tongue and looked away. Then she shrugged. "I'm trying not to be such a downer, but it's been tough. And this is the first really good news I've had in a while."

He wrapped his arm around her and squeezed her shoulder. "You deserve it, Bailey. I'm happy for you."

She let his words wash over her and hoped they might at least be partly true. She didn't feel like she deserved much of anything, but she knew Gracie did, and so she hoped things might keep looking up for the two of them.

Judy brought them a piece of chocolate cake without asking.

"Oh, and this. This is unmatched anywhere, too." She took the first bite, aware that Maverick watched her lick the chocolate from her lips. And then a new, thrilling kind of jitter crept in. Their tradition when eating this cake: she always kissed the last bite from his lips.

But obviously that wouldn't be happening now. Would it?

Maverick seemed nonplussed. He grabbed a spoon. "You better hurry, or I'm gonna eat the whole thing."

"Oh no, you don't." She pretended to fight back his spoon and took the biggest bite she could manage. "Mmm. Really, this is so good."

They ate a few more bites, but Maverick seemed distracted. "So, the Dawson Ranch sponsors a team of 4-H kids in the upcoming fair. I was watching Gracie with the pigs, and I wondered would she want to participate?"

Bailey's eyes widened. "She would love that more than anything. Could she really?"

"Of course. We'll add her to the team and get them started on their new piglets in a couple weeks. Good timing, really."

"I can't wait to tell her."

One more bite waited on their plate. He scooped it up, and his knowing eyes peered into hers. "Some traditions are harder to let go than others." He lifted his napkin to wipe the frosting from his lips, and a part of her wilted inside.

Maverick paid for their meal, and when they stood to leave, he hesitated. "Come over. You and Gracie and your parents. Mama's been asking. We'll do our Sunday dinner like we used to."

"Okay. Tomorrow?"

"Yes. Let's start tomorrow. All the guys are in town for the rodeo still. We can catch Nash before he takes off."

"I'd like that. Thank you." She watched his face, trying to get a read on him. "You ever gonna ride again?"

"I did, remember."

"I know, and I saw your face. I know how much you loved it."

He shrugged. "Sometimes we don't get to pursue our dreams."

She knew it was a pointed comment, and she deserved it. "But do you wish you could?"

He looked away. "I didn't think I did." He shook his head. "This feels nice, actually, to be able to talk to someone about all this."

She waited for him to continue.

"As soon as I put the gear back on, I wanted back into that life more than almost anything."

She placed a hand on his arm, stepping close. "Then you should, Maverick. You should."

He shrugged. "I said *almost* anything. There is one thing I want more."

"To take care of your father's ranch."

"Yes. No amount of rodeo fame would ever make up for letting the ranch fail."

"I see that." And she admired Maverick even more. "But I still think there's room for both. Or there should be."

"I won't deny I've thought about it over and over, but now's not the time."

She didn't know when he would ever feel like it was the time. But she hoped that someday he would. She knew it was a selfish desire. If he got to achieve his dreams, it would make up in a small part for her deserting them all, leaving him to be the responsible one while she pursued and failed at her dreams.

He led her out of the diner. They waved goodbye to Judy. "Now I want to take the truck up to the lake."

"What?" Were they going to visit all their old haunts? "I'd love that. Is the rope swing still there?"

"Of course. We go up now and then to make sure of it."

"Then let's go!"

Maverick whooped, and they raced to his truck. She hopped in just like she always had, swinging up and landing on her backside. He shut the door after her, and she enjoyed the smile that lit his whole face while he made his way around to the driver's side.

He peeled out of the parking lot like they were kids, and she rolled down the windows. The music came on, and she recognized their playlist. A love ballad from their favorite band started up.

"Hey, that's not even fair."

"Who said anything about playing fair?"

She shook her head. "Maverick Dawson, you have to know what I'm thinking about right now."

"Prom."

"Which one?"

"Let's see. 'Endearing charms?' You're thinking of our first prom." He wiggled his eyebrows. "And maybe a few other firsts."

"Of course, I am. How does this help our friend status?"

"Oh, I didn't say we both *felt* like friends. It's hard to backtrack those kinds of feelings." He eyed her. "At least for me." His expression said he was fishing. But she wasn't ready to admit to anything. She was certain he'd never want her back, and she wasn't sure she could handle being at his side again, knowing all that she'd done to hurt him and his family. But as she looked into his handsome goodness, she realized she might want just that, no matter the cost. But she wasn't ready to admit such a thing out loud. If she did, she might jinx it.

"I think it's pretty safe to assume I'll always have feelings for you."

His face clouded with disappointment.

She regretted a missed opportunity. "You have to know that leaving broke my heart. Not loving you was never the problem."

He turned away, and his truck moved up a smaller dirt road toward the entrance to the lake path. "Here we go! Look, the road is overgrown; let's close the windows."

They drove through overhanging branches that brushed against the truck as they made their way up the mountain road.

"It's all so beautiful. And it smells good!" She cracked her window. "I dreamed of this smell. I remember lying in my bed, pretending I didn't have anything to worry about because you and I were driving up to the lake."

His face filled with pain, and she regretted her words again. She wasn't sure what exactly had hurt him, but she tried to mend things. "Are you gonna jump in?"

"You're gonna go there?"

"Well, yeah…"

"You know the rules about swimming?"

"I do."

His eyes twinkled with a wicked glint. "I don't know if you can handle it."

She dipped her head back and laughed. Then she eyed him, slowly, deliciously, from his thigh to the top of his head. And he watched her do it. Then she said, "You might be right."

He laughed. "I see that look. You know I can still see what you're thinking sometimes."

"Oh, can you?"

"Yes, I can. And I'll just tell you now, it's way too cold for swimming. But...if I can see that look on your face again, I'll gladly come back up here this spring." He reached for her hand. "If you'll swim with me."

She just swallowed, not trusting herself to speak. They continued on in a companionable silence. She still wanted to ask his advice, but she didn't dare talk about her ex when things were so comfortable, or at least hopeful, between them.

Had he forgiven her? She couldn't tell. She'd hurt him, but he was willing to be friends. And that was worth so much more to her than even she could have guessed. She opened her mouth, trying to force a conversation about Daniel, but one of their all-time favorite songs came up. She belted it out with Maverick at her side. They laughed all the way through the chorus and she thought maybe bringing back old times was even better than talking about new ones.

Chapter 10

Maverick turned his truck up the small path in the brush to get to the lake, happy to be heading up there with Bailey beside him.

"Talk to me about your dad," Bailey prompted.

"You know Dad. He was the best."

"I know, but…" She seemed troubled.

"What is it?"

"He was everything to you boys, wasn't he?"

"Yeah. I spend a lot of time reminding myself I'm not as good as he was."

"No, Maverick, you can't do that. You're awesome. You're comparing yourself to the dad he became, not the dad he started out as."

He didn't say anything for a few minutes.

"I was there. At the funeral."

"What!"

"Yeah. Gracie and I hid in the balcony choir seats. I was lucky she didn't fuss."

He couldn't believe what he was hearing. "You know

what I wanted most in the world that day?" He saw her wince. "To see you. Hear you. Anything."

She looked away. "I'm sorry."

It didn't help either of them to keep circling back to her apologizing. But it felt good for him to express his hurt, and she needed to know. "Why the questions about my dad?" Something was on her mind. He could see the wheels spinning. "You've done a remarkable job with Gracie on your own. She's doing fine, and you've got your parents now."

She nodded.

"But I feel empty without my dad. It's different. The world lost a lodestone for me."

The air was thick with expectation. Did he want to jump in and save her and Gracie, fill in as the dad she needed for her child? Of course. But he didn't know if that was the right choice for him. Not yet, anyway. This conversation would blow his whole plan to be friends way out of the water.

"And you've got the Dawson family. Look at all the men in this child's life. She's not gonna stand a chance at finding someone to marry, not unless the guy is Dawson-quality."

Bailey laughed. "And that's about near impossible to find anywhere. Maybe Nash would wait around for her."

Maverick tipped his head back and laughed in surprise. "You know, he just might. Mama says he has no interest in marrying anyone right now."

They pulled up to the lake, and Maverick groaned. Tiff's truck was parked in his spot.

"Is that—" Bailey's tone let him know how much she wasn't gonna like his answer.

"Tiff."

"The devil herself." She frowned, put her feet up on his dash, and crossed her arms.

"Hey, now. Come on. She's been through a lot."

"She's not any nicer now than she was in high school. She's still out to get me. You should have heard her at the rodeo."

"She's never had it as good as you have."

"That's not even fair. It might have been true when we were kids, but my life hasn't been roses, Maverick. And I've learned a few things. One of them is that I don't have to put up with any haters in my life."

"Fair enough, but—"

A scream interrupted him, and he leapt out of the truck, taking off down the ravine path toward their swimming hole. Adrenaline raced through his body. A part of him registered the sound of Bailey coming behind him. That comforted him. If something was really wrong at the water, they'd need to work together to get help. And there weren't too many people he'd rather have at his back than Bailey.

One time in high school, when they were out on the football field, one of the guys collapsed. Bailey had run out to him, beating the medical staff. She'd immediately run back to the stands, once they'd begun easing off his helmet, to tell his parents that he was conscious and breathing.

He rounded the corner, and the water came into view. His pace picked up, and his breathing hitched when he saw a splash of bright red on the rocks at the side of the water.

"Tiff!" he shouted.

"Maverick? Oh, Maverick! I'm here!" Her voice sounded strong.

He pushed through the last brush and almost ran into Tiff holding her head. Blood dripped down her face.

"Whoa there, Tiff." He reached out to steady her, and she let herself collapse into his arms.

"I'm so glad you're here. I don't know what to do."

"Are you alone?"

"No, but they're no use."

Her two friends were up here with her. She pointed to a trail of vodka bottles and her two girlfriends sitting back up against a rock in a daze.

"This is ridiculously dangerous." He pulled off his shirt, and her eyes widened as she openly checked him out.

Bailey approached. "Oh no, you've got to put some pressure on that."

He held up his shirt, and Bailey stretched it taut while he ripped off pieces. He handed the first to Tiff. "Put this up against your cut, right there."

She held the ball of fabric up against the cut, her pout coming on strong. She scowled at Bailey. "What's she doing here?"

"We're hiking the rim." He didn't have time for whatever spat they had going between them. Bailey ripped a few more strips and tied them together without him asking. Then he wrapped it around Tiff's head, holding the first wad of fabric in place to hopefully stop the bleeding. "What happened?"

"Oh, you know. We were just messing around. I jumped off the high rock, but I slipped."

He shook his head. "We've got to get you three out of here. Do you think they can walk?"

She shrugged and then swayed.

"How much have you had?"

"I'm not drunk. Well, maybe legally I am, but I can walk."

He looked her over. "Does anything else hurt?"

"Nah. I'm fine now that you're here." She leaned into him, giggling.

Maverick steadied her. "Let's get you over there by your friends."

When he leaned down to help her get situated, she pulled him forward. He was off-balance and tipped to the side so that he was lying in her lap. "Hey now." He smiled. "That's not the kind of outing I'm on."

"You've never complained before."

He gritted his teeth at her false insinuation.

Bailey huffed behind him. "Well, I can see you might be a while. I think I'll take the trail myself."

He lifted himself up off Tiff and saluted. "You ladies stay put now. We'll be back to check on you."

Bailey was already almost at the turn of the trail. He made his way toward her. She had no right to even care what he'd done while she was gone. But it made him grin. She cared. And that made him unreasonably happy.

"What are you grinning about back there?" She waited for him, one hand on her hip.

"What's got you all bothered?" He chuckled when she turned from him and kept marching up the ravine.

After a moment, he called, "You gonna let me catch up?"

She paused but didn't say anything.

When at last he was walking at her side, she smiled. "Everything's the same up here. Just look at how beautiful it all is."

They walked a few more feet and stopped to touch their

tree. It was a habit. They did it every time they reached this spot. It seemed unnatural not to. They'd carved their initials on the back side of the tree. He knew they were still there, but she didn't move to look at them. Neither said a word. He reached for her hand, and she let him entwine their fingers.

"How's your mama been?" she asked.

He smiled. "She's one strong woman. It's been hard on her, having Dad gone. Hard on us all. But she rules the family just as she always has, and I'm happy the guys respect her."

"And you. They all look to you."

He shrugged. "Sometimes I wonder if it might be good for them to have to stand on their own sometime."

"Don't they?"

"They do. But maybe not like they could. When everything fell to me, I learned some things. Like if I don't do the finances, they don't get done. If I don't make sure the cows get purchased, or sold, or open the back pasture at the right time, or harvest the hay, we lose money. If I don't call the family in for holidays or meetings or whenever Mama wants to talk to them..." He kicked a rock. "You learn some things when you're the man in charge."

"Like, what it feels like to never do that last rodeo circuit?"

He looked out over the widening view. "Like that."

"Decker does the horses, right?"

"Yeah. But even that falls to me sometimes. 'Cause he takes off."

"And he does his own circuit too, right?"

"Yep."

She squeezed his hand. "You're a good man, Maverick. I'm proud of what you've got going here."

He nodded. But her questions and his complaining were making him doubt again his ability or determination to keep his father's ranch alive. And that was a dangerous place for him. Riding that bull had felt too good. And seeing Bailey here had reignited old feelings, not just for her but for his days on the circuit with her in the stands. And suddenly, for the first time in a long time, he started wanting something for himself.

They crested the top of the ravine at last, and they both turned to face the valley. Maverick looked toward his father's land, like he always did. He was proud of the neat patchwork fields, the beautiful homestead. The Dawson ranch had been around since his great-grandfather helped settle the valley. And he was proud to be a part of that, proud of his dad and the work he'd done to make the ranch a thriving entity.

Bailey watched him. He felt her gaze, his body humming in response. But when he turned to her, he was surprised by the intensity of the feeling he saw in her face. She shook her head. "I'm sorry, Maverick. I'm sorry for what I did to you." Her eyes welled up.

"Hey, now, I thought we got through this."

She shook her head and turned away.

He stepped closer. "Come here." He pulled her into his arms, his hands running up and down her back. Oh, he'd missed this, missed her. Everything seemed to click back into alignment with her at his side. "We're a good team, you know."

She nodded against him. "I should have never left. I ruined the most perfect thing I may ever know."

"It's not ruined. Look at us now." His heart pounded against her. Did he dare tell her what he longed to say? Could he risk his heart again with the woman who had all the power over his happiness?

She lifted her chin. "I want to be as good a friend to you as you are to me."

He brushed a piece of hair from her face. "Friends." His eyes held hers, and he stared deeply, comfortably, into the face of the woman he thought he'd known. "I'm sorry for underestimating you. Sorry I never championed your dreams."

"I'm sorry I never told you what they were."

"Hey, we were kids."

She shook her head. "I'm gonna grow up and make it up to everyone. I'll do right by Gracie and my parents, and you…" Her face crumpled as if the weight of it all might press her into the ground.

"No, no, hon. That's not how it works."

She lifted her chin. "That's what my parents said, too, but…"

He tightened his arms around her, wishing he could hug away all the worry of her heart. "What you did broke a lot of hearts. I'm not gonna sugarcoat it. But you were hurting too. And you came back. We all just need to take some time to heal. We're not doing this alone you know."

She sniffed. "You talking about letting God in."

"Yeah, remember what it says in Isaiah in the Bible. "He was bruised for our iniquities. He carried our sorrows." He tucked a flyaway hair behind her ear even though the wind was bound send it flying again. "You don't have to run around trying to fix all our wounds. You just need to do what you're doing, reaching out, loving. I'm sure your parents are just happy to have you back in their lives and to know Gracie Faith. And God does the rest."

She nodded. "Does He?"

"He sure does. The best part about that verse is the end. With His stripes, we are healed."

"And we're supposed to just give it all to him?"

"Well, you repent, right? You try to do good. But if you accept Him as your Savior, if you have Faith in His love for you, then yes, you're supposed to give it all to Him." As he said the words, he know he was talking right to himself, that every word was meant for him just as much as Bailey."

"When did you get so smart?"

He laughed. "I'm not. But give yourself a break. I've got to work through my own stuff with all this."

"I know. I think it's gonna take me some time for both of us."

"Yep. I think so too."

"And you, trying to make me feel better about something terrible I did to you. It just isn't fair, Maverick. Something good's got to come your way too."

He stared down into her wide and caring eyes and then shook his head. "I've already got lots of good pouring down on me. I'm happy as a pig in mud."

She laughed. "You sound like your dad."

"I've never heard better words of praise."

"I miss him."

He nodded. "You know, there is something you could do to make up for all the pain you caused us."

She lifted her head. "What?"

"There's these candies with pecans and caramel…"

"Maverick." She whacked him. "You want me to make you some turtles? Is that it?"

"Well, yeah, no one makes them like you do, and you've been gone for five years. How much longer does a man have to wait?"

She laughed, a soft, comfortable sound, and Maverick started to feel a bit better hearing it.

"I'll bring them to dinner tomorrow, along with whatever else my mama says we should bring."

"She'll bring boysenberry pie."

"And how do you know?"

"Because she knows it's my favorite."

"She been spoiling you while I'm gone?"

"I can't help it if the woman loves me like her own son."

Bailey rested her cheek against his chest again. "I think she looks at you that way."

"Just like my mama thinks of you as her daughter."

As they stood at the top of the ridge, looking out over everything Maverick loved, his heart began to hope. Maybe, finally, things were coming back together.

Chapter 11

A lodestone. Bailey frowned on their way over to the Dawson house for dinner. Not having his dad in his life tore at Maverick. He felt lost without him. Is that what Gracie would feel? Bailey replayed Daniel's conversation in her mind over and over. She wasn't any closer to figuring out what to do about him. Was it better to have a dad, no matter how crummy? Had Daniel changed any?

Bailey and her mama carried half their kitchen into the Dawson house.

"Not sure the Dawsons need to cook at all with what you women brought over." Bailey's dad shook his head. "You sure they're needing all this food?"

Maverick's mom stepped into the entryway. "Of course, we're needing all this, Earl. Have you seen all these mouths to feed?" She grabbed a couple trays. "Nash, come help the Hempsteads."

He ran up and picked up a couple items from Bailey's hands. "Oh, someone's gonna be as pleased as we've ever seen him."

"Oh?" Maverick's mama looked over then smiled. "You made the turtles." She nodded. "Now that's the way."

Bailey grinned. Maverick's mama always said the way to win over her boys was through cooking them something special. And in some ways, Bailey guessed she was right. The Dawson Mama had certainly mastered keeping her boys well fed, healthy, and happy. Bailey wished to be even a tiny bit of the mother this woman was.

They spread everything out on the serving bar just as Maverick came in with a tray full of steaks. "Well, if that isn't the prettiest picture I've ever seen."

Mrs. Dawson called out, "Nash, ring the dinner bell."

Bailey smiled in anticipation, waiting. The clanging rang out over the valley. And she heard her heart pound in response. When the Dawson dinner bell rang, you knew good things were about to happen.

Everyone gathered in and found a place at the table. They'd added a couple leaves so every person had a place. They even brought in a beautiful wood stool for Gracie to sit on. When at last the group was settled, Bailey looked out over everyone. She sat at Maverick's left at the head of the table. Gracie sat next to her. Bailey met his gaze, and everything shifted one more notch toward being all right in the world as she looked around at everyone she loved all in one place. Except for Maverick's dad. It was hard for her, being here and not seeing him. Everyone else missed him too, probably worse than she did, but she hadn't had time to mourn him yet. Mr. Dawson's mighty presence was notably absent in this great family meeting. She reached over and placed her hand in Maverick's big one. "I miss your dad."

He nodded. "Thank you."

Everyone was gathered. The twins—Decker and Dylan

—Nash, Bailey, her parents, Maverick, his mama, and now Gracie Faith. And it felt like one giant family. Her smile grew, and she didn't even try to dim it, no matter that she felt silly.

Maverick grinned in response. "This is pretty great having everyone here together like this, isn't it?"

"It sure is," his mama called out from the other end of the table. "And now, I just want to say a few words. We're so glad to have the Hempsteads with us for Sunday dinners again. It feels like everything is as it should be once again." She looked up to the picture above the mantel, the last one taken before Mr. Dawson had passed away. Bailey was in it. Her hand squeezed Maverick's again.

His mama continued. "We always miss your father when we gather like this. And we know the family just isn't complete without him, but it will be much more so when each of these boys finds himself a good woman."

The guys all made middle school noises about the idea of girls until their mama hushed them again. "Now, I'm serious about this, boys. It's high time you were settling down." She adjusted her fork then looked up with a big smile. "We're so happy to have the newest member of the Dawson-Hempstead family. Gracie Faith. Welcome to the family, my dear."

"Thank you." Her wide eyes took everyone in.

"Maverick, will you pray?"

"Yes Ma'am."

Maverick's deep confident voice turned humble as he bowed his head, his words steady and sure. "Dear God...."

When he finished, Bailey wiped her eyes. She loved this man.

"And now." Mrs. Dawson smiled. "Let's eat."

"Let's eat," they all chorused.

In the quiet while everyone took their first bite, little Gracie Faith said, "I like these people, Mama."

The whole room burst into laughter.

"We like you too, Gracie." Maverick held out his fist, and Gracie fist-bumped him.

Bailey exchanged looks with her parents. Their love for little Gracie was so evident, Bailey knew she'd done the right thing. Things were working out better than she'd hoped. Everyone was together, they'd forgiven her, and they were happy. With so many good men in her life, did Gracie really need someone like Daniel?

Long after dinner was cleaned up and Gracie had dozed off on the couch with her grandpa, Maverick and Bailey sat together on their favorite porch swing. Both of their houses had the same swing sitting on the back porch, filled with pillows. Maverick had brought a blanket outside for them to share, and they swung together gently, watching the stars come out one by one.

"That was awesome." Bailey shook her head. How could she have left something so incredible?

"What? Having everyone together like that?"

"Yeah. And for Gracie Faith to have that…" She couldn't speak for the emotion that welled up in her throat. "Oh my word, Maverick, in all the time you've known me, have I ever teared up as much as you've seen in the last week?"

He shook his head. "Nope. But I don't know what kind of woman you'd be if you weren't getting emotional at all the beautiful things going on. Did you see Gracie playing with my brothers?"

"I did." She watched him for a moment. "But the best

thing I saw today was you and Gracie sitting together by the fireplace, reading books."

He chuckled. "That little girl loves her books."

"She does. It was our time together. When I had two jobs and auditions and all the other stuff that kept me from spending time with her, reading books was our time. And I'd read as long as she wanted, most of the time she'd have to nudge me awake to turn the page, but I sat there and loved every second until she fell asleep." She shook her head. "It made my heart happy, seeing you two reading together."

"You're a real good mama, Bailey, just like I knew you'd be." His fingers brushed along her shoulder, absently running circles over her skin. The motion sent a rush of tingles through her.

She wished it were true, that she was a real good mama. "I think I'll get there. We're doing much better since I came home."

"And that's what it's all about, right? Getting better, doing better. Gracie is one amazing kid, and that's all because of you." He started kneading out the knots in her neck.

"Oh, that's heaven."

"Did you forget my talent?"

"No way. I longed for this."

He worked on her neck, and Bailey thought she might pass out from the awesome sensation that ran through her. "When I look in her eyes, I see you. In her voice, I hear you. She's so beautiful. She's her own person and so much of you all at the same time. It's awesome to see."

His warm thoughts washed over her. Her body came

alive with desire, craving his hands on her. She searched his face and suddenly felt a little bold and a touch brazen.

She leaned into him. "Hey, wanna go see if the moon is out back behind the barn?"

His gaze flitted to hers. He paused, eyeing her. "Yeah, I sure do." He reached for her hand. "Do you?"

She laced her fingers in his. "I wouldn't have asked if I didn't."

He stood and then knelt down. "Here, climb up on my back."

"You sure?"

"Absolutely. I'm in no mood for you to go changing your mind. Let's hurry."

She laughed and climbed up on his back. As soon as she was situated, he took off running, tossing the blanket over his shoulder for her to carry. She wrapped her hands around his neck and clung to him. Could it be possible for them to have a healthy relationship? Oh, she hoped so. It wouldn't be what they had before. But maybe something more. Something better.

He tore across their yard, raced around the back side of the barn, and climbed up into the loft. He laid the blanket out so they could sit on it. And they stared out the back of the barn, waiting.

"It should be rising any minute." Bailey pointed to the sky.

"Oh, I'm in no hurry." Maverick leaned back on his elbows, eyeing her like he had when they were young.

"You aren't?" She leaned back so she was right next to him.

"Nope." He lifted himself up on an elbow so that their faces were close. She could see every well-known freckle and the soft smile lines that had shown up since she left. His jawline was strong, his teeth beautiful; his eyes sparkled at her. But there was something there besides just his goodness. A yearning she only now noticed. Seeing his pain so bare in his eyes, she wanted to replace all his sorrow with something good, with her love, with happiness, with anything she could give him.

He lifted her hand in his. "When you look at me like that, I feel like I could do anything in the world."

"How am I looking at you?" She ran her fingers down along his jawline.

"Like you love me." He pressed his lips to the tips of her fingers. "Like you'd do anything for me. I see it all in your face. And I don't deserve it." He pulled one of her fingertips into his mouth. "But I'll take it."

She shifted closer. "You can see all of that just by looking?"

"Yep." He reached out and teased a piece of hay out of her hair.

"What else do you see?" She widened her eyes and tried to let him see into her heart.

"That you're wanting to be kissed by someone who knows how."

"You can see that too?" Her voice sounded breathless even to her own ears. But she couldn't deny it. She'd never wanted to kiss Maverick Dawson so much in her life.

He lightly ran a hand down her hair, pulling pieces back, shifting them behind her shoulder. Every touch sent a ripple of pleasure through her.

"You loved me before."

She closed her eyes against the pain of his words. "I've

never stopped loving you." She knew what he wanted to know, to understand.

"But you left anyway."

She opened her eyes.

His hands continued playing with her hair, and she would have done anything in that moment to erase all the sadness she'd ever caused him. "I won't leave ever again."

He studied her face, searched deep into her eyes.

"I'm not asking for anything from you. I'm happy to be back in your life, to be friends, for my little girl to know so many good people. But I'm not leaving, either, and you should know that."

He moved closer and pressed his lips to her forehead. "I'm happy to hear that, 'cause nothing around here is special unless you're a part of it." A soothing warmth spread through her. This was right. This was Maverick. This was everything she'd been missing.

Then he wrapped an arm around her back and cradled her underneath his chin. "So, what happens if I do what we both want to do right now?"

She raised an eyebrow. "Since when did you start talking about everything? We'd have been making out with the moon overhead by now—"

He pressed his lips to hers. And that ended any plans she had about trying to keep things platonic. Whatever he did, whatever he wanted, she was in. And that was that. She wrapped her arms around his back, pulling him as close as he could go. He started slow, caressing her with his soft, velvety mouth. He tasted the same as she remembered. He smelled the same. He kissed the same. And all of it filled her with longing for more.

She responded to his insistence, trying to capture his

lower lip, pressing her mouth to his over and over until everything else went away and all she wanted was him. He shifted, rising above her, and his kisses became more urgent. It was all she could do to not call out for more.

But he slowed. She caught her breath. And at length, he breathed out against her with his forehead resting on hers. "Wow, Bailey."

"Yeah."

"Why did you go, again?"

"I was an idiot."

He nodded. "So, um. Friends?" His stomach shook.

"Yeeaaah. Friends." She laughed with him. "Hey, we can be whatever you want us to be. Call it what you like. I'm not going anywhere."

He grinned. "Well, now I know what I want us to be doing."

She pushed his shoulder, and he rolled to the side so she could sit up beside him. "Did we miss the moon?"

"Have we ever caught it?"

"No way." She ran a hand down his arm. "Hey, thanks for all this. For not hating me."

"I can't hate you. Even when I wanted to hate you, I couldn't."

She nodded.

"Hey, Maaaav!" Nash's loud call made them both snort.

"What!" Maverick called down.

"I've got a little princess here who wants to see the magic moon with her mama."

"Gracie, are you down there?"

"Yeah! Mama, is there a moon up there with you?"

She shook her head, and she and Maverick crawled to the end of the platform and looked down.

Nash tipped his hat. "I see Bailey there is sufficiently mussed up. Nice work."

"What!" Bailey patted her hair and then gave up. "Anyway…"

Maverick called down, "There's no moon up here. We missed it."

Nash snorted.

"But how about we come down and I show you what we're gonna be doing with your new baby pig."

Her mouth opened so wide Bailey was sure it might never close. "My new pig! Mama! Do I get a new baby pig?"

"You sure do, honey. Maverick said he's gonna help you learn to be a pig boss."

Maverick grimaced. "Except that's not what we call it. You're gonna train your own pig and enter it in the fair."

She took off running around the grassy space behind the barn, shouting.

"Thanks, Nash." Bailey turned to climb down the ladder.

"I'm just happy to see some of this going on. We're all behind you two no matter what."

When she got to the bottom, she turned and wrapped her arms around a surprised Nash. "Thank you."

He patted her back once, twice, then stepped away. "Backing away. See." He held his hands out.

"Whatever." Bailey shook her head.

"Nah, I know. No matter what happens, you're family. Just wanted you to know."

Maverick clapped a hand on his shoulder. "Thanks, brother."

Gracie ran up with her hands in the air, and when she

got to Maverick, she jumped as high as she could up into his arms.

Luckily, Maverick knew what she was after and swung her up into the air before sitting her at his hip. "You ready to meet your baby pig's mama?"

"Ooooh. Yes."

Bailey watched as Maverick explained all about the mama pig and how the babies were waiting to come into the world until they were big and ready. He went on and on, and Bailey drank in every word, watching the fascination grow in Gracie's face. Bailey imagined many a fall just like this one. She let her mind wander to when there would be a few more children around, to gatherings with the brothers and their wives and her parents, and it all felt too wonderful to be true.

She knew she had to hang on before it all slipped through her fingers.

Chapter 12

Maverick should be congratulating himself on a super fine make-out session with a hot woman, but it wasn't just any woman; it was Bailey. And now that he'd kissed her again, his whole body remembered she was his woman. Not a friend—no way. She was the woman he wanted to stand by his side in everything.

When she'd asked him if he wanted to go watch the moon, he could have said no. He knew what was coming. And then the magic of the night air, her eyes shining up at him, and her words, "I won't leave ever again." It was too much to resist.

But now he had to deal with the consequences. Could he trust her with his heart? His brain said there was no way he should ever do that again, but she already owned every beat of his heart, so now what? As he watched her with little Gracie, he had to ask himself, what did he love? The relationship they used to have? Or the new Bailey?

Big Mama Lulu, their sow, grunted and fell to her side.

Her breathing started to get real heavy, and Bailey gasped beside him. "Is she?"

He chuckled. "I think so." He leaned in real close and rested the top of his hat on Bailey's head. "Do we tell her, or do we sneak out and pretend like nothing's going on?"

"I can hear you." Gracie's little voice surprised him.

"Not much gets past my girl."

He turned to see Gracie with both hands on her hips, watching him.

Then he looked from Bailey to Gracie. "I think Grandma has some yummy dessert going on back at the house. You ready for boysenberry pie?"

Bailey laughed. "I have a feeling Maverick's ready for some of that pie."

"You know I am. I already ate the turtles."

"What? All of them?"

"Well, no, but the others I hid in my room." He winked. "And I think we have some ice cream, specially made."

Gracie started to skip out the door, but then she stopped. "But what's going on with Lulu?"

"See? Catches everything." Bailey grinned. "Nothing, honey. Well, nothing we're sure of. Sometimes when mamas are pregnant, they get real tired and rest like that."

"But sometimes they do this when they're about to have the little piggies come out."

"Come out?" Gracie's eyes went wide.

"Now you've done it."

He felt his cheeks warm. "Well, I didn't want to be leaving out parts."

"That's what talking to kids is all about. You leave out parts."

He laughed. "Well, not when *I* talk to kids." He held

out his hand. "Come here, pumpkin. I'm gonna teach you something really cool about pigs."

Bailey shook her head. "This I gotta see."

Gracie ran up and climbed on his lap, and Bailey sat beside him. "See Lulu over there?" The big sow moaned. "She's gonna start having some babies tonight."

Gracie wrinkled up her nose like she didn't understand.

"Right now, they're all living inside her. But they're too big for that little space, and they're gonna come out and live outside now."

"How long's this gonna take?"

"I don't know. Sometimes it takes all night long."

"So can I come back tomorrow and take a look?"

"That's a great idea. I see you're practical like your mama. Then we can go in and get me some of that pie."

She hopped off his lap. "Can I really have one of the babies?"

"You sure can. As soon as they're old enough, we'll work together to get it ready to show."

She grabbed one of each of their hands and skipped between them back toward the house.

They made their way back, both their mamas looking out at them from the kitchen window. Maverick knew they painted a pretty picture. He knew they were filling everyone inside that house with all kinds of hope. And he loved them all for it. But he sure hoped nobody's heart was gonna be broken through all this.

They ate dessert, played games, and laughed more than they had in a long time. Then at last, they walked the Hempsteads out to their car.

"Thank you for a real nice time." Mama Hempstead

kissed Maverick's cheek, hugged his mama, and climbed up into the car while her husband held the door.

Mama's eyes crinkled with a happiness you only earned by living like she did. "I'm so happy Sunday dinners are back. You join us as often as you can, now."

"We will, Mama Dawson." Bailey stepped over and wrapped her arms around the woman she loved like her own mama.

"Oh, it feels good to hear you calling me that again. Welcome back, honey."

"Thank you."

Then Maverick opened the door for Gracie to climb in. "Get buckled, little lady."

Her small voice made him smile. "Okay."

Bailey stepped closer, his arm still on the door. She stood on her toes and kissed him on the mouth right in front of everyone. He was too shocked to respond. She stepped away quickly, her face uncertain, so he reached an arm around her and pulled her back. "Well, if we're gonna go announcing things to the loved ones, we best be doing it right."

Then he kissed her again, with emphasis.

The guys called out from the front door, and his mama clapped.

They laughed, and then Bailey climbed into her car.

He closed the door, wishing she was staying with him instead of heading back to her place, even if it was just over the ridge.

His mama came to stand by him as they drove away. "You okay?"

"I'm about as okay as a horse who doesn't know what's good for him."

"She's a good soul."

"I know that."

"Perhaps a bit skittish."

"That's one of the things I'm worried about."

She nodded. "But she knows where home is."

"Yeah, she came back. Thanks for dinner, Mama. It was real special."

"Your papa would have liked it too."

"Yeah, he would have."

They turned to go into the house. As soon as they entered the front door, Decker waved an envelope at him.

"What's this?"

"Something awesome. Since we're all here, let's talk about it."

"Well, okay then." He made his way into the living room. His other brothers were already in there.

"Does everyone but me know what's going on?"

"We sure do." Nash grinned.

Decker stood at the front of the room. "If you could please be seated. This next meeting of the Dawson family is now in session."

Maverick sat by his mama, and he couldn't tell if she knew what was going on.

"I have here an offer addressed to Maverick."

Maverick held up his hand. "Well now, if it's addressed to me…"

"Steady. I'll give it to you in just a minute. But this offer is for a spot on a rodeo team, to ride the circuit—"

"What? Give that here." Maverick stood and took it from him. After a quick perusal, he saw Decker wasn't kidding. His old team wanted him back, no strings, no penalties. They just wanted him to ride bulls.

"You could do it, Maverick," Nash said.

"Not with everyone else doing circuits of their own."

"Well, we were thinking maybe we could take turns."

Mama rested a hand on his arm. "And I could hire a manager."

Maverick's first reaction was to shake his head at that. No one but a Dawson had ever run the ranch, and he was pretty sure no one else could. But then he let the idea settle, and he recognized it had merit. Even if he didn't ride the circuit, a manager might be a great idea.

"So this spring, you guys think you could take care of everything while I take off?"

"Believe it or not, we could." Decker shook his head. "And every one of us thinks it's time you got to do something you love, too."

The guys all watched him, open, sincere, willing to give up a little bit of something of their own so he could have a circuit. He knew what it would cost them. If they stepped away when things were hot, sometimes they just couldn't get back in. For those of them who didn't have a record or a really winning season, they might not be able to get back on a team. Though sometimes just being a Dawson gave them a leg up.

"I don't know."

"We figure, by spring, you and Bailey might already be a thing, and she could go along with the little peanut."

"You thought of that, did you?" He knew they meant well. He was grateful. Touched. But he couldn't do it this year. "Look, guys…"

"No. Don't say it. Just think about it. Stick the envelope on top of your desk and mull it over." Nash stood. "And I'm gonna go hit the hay. G'night, brothers. Mama."

"Good night," they chorused.

And soon, Maverick and his mama were the only ones left sitting in their chairs, staring at a packet of papers.

"What do you think I should do, Mama?"

"You'll know what to do. I don't have any easy answers for this one. But it's nice to have an option. If you need to get away, this is a great opportunity."

He wondered at the way she'd phrased things. But he just nodded.

"Hey, guys!" he called loud enough for them to hear him upstairs. "I've got something more to say."

When his brothers lined the stairs, Nash in his pajama bottoms and Decker with a toothbrush in his mouth, Maverick grinned. "I think we should consider a new Dawson presence at the Texas state fair."

His mama sucked in her breath. And his brothers' eyes lit.

He knew that would get them off him and onto something awesome.

Decker leaned on the stair railing. "What do you have in mind?"

"I just think our Jersey cow needs to make a showing."

"Okay…and?" Nash was too into his own self for his own good, but Maverick couldn't blame him.

"And I think we should do a Dawson rodeo demonstration."

"A show?"

"Absolutely. I think we should pitch our show."

"You know they'll take us."

"Well, of course."

"And I think we should take the 4-H kids."

The brothers exchanged glances.

"What?"

"So is this about us or the cute little daughter of your hottie girlfriend?"

Maverick laughed. "This is all about you. It's always about you. Now, if Gracie Faith happens to win her second blue ribbon while we're at it, I'm gonna call that a big ol' bonus for Uncle Maverick."

They shook their heads, every one of them, in imitation of their father. But each one of their eyes twinkled like this was the best idea he'd ever had.

"Okay, so I'm taking that as a yes. Decker, get us signed up."

"What? Why me?"

"'Cause you're the one that got me the rodeo paperwork."

He pointed his finger at the other brothers. "I knew this was gonna come back to nip at me. Entering the state fair takes months."

"Let us know when we're all signed up and ready to go."

He moaned, but Maverick could tell they were all pleased.

"And you, Mama."

"What about me?"

"Are you gonna enter any of your quilts?"

She started to shake her head no but then paused. "You know, I just might make a new one."

"That's excellent. I think this is gonna be the best Texas state fair showing we've had in years."

"There's just one more thing I gotta know." Dylan raised his hand.

"Yes."

"Just how long were you tangled up with Bailey before Nash came out to interrupt you?"

Maverick laughed. "I don't know what you're talking about. We were watching the moon rise."

"We could always go watch the footage..." For a moment, his mama's expression looked just as mischievous as Nash's. Maverick understood how she got on with her youngest son so well.

"What footage?" Maverick cringed.

"The footage from the camera your daddy had installed up there when we were worried about critters. We used to scroll through the files, and let me tell you, we saw a lot more than critters up there."

The brothers all turned to look at their mama with the same horrified expressions until she started to shake and held a hand over her face as she laughed, tears streaming down her cheeks. She waved her hand. "I'm just messing with you boys. But now I'm beginning to think I should have done just that."

They each kissed her cheek as they turned to go, laughing off her comment.

"Good night, boys." She waved them off to bed.

Maverick followed them, feeling happier than he had in a long time. Even the tiny voice inside that whispered things couldn't be as good as they seemed was drowned out by the memory of holding Bailey in his arms.

Chapter 13

Bailey went home happier than she'd been since before leaving Willow Creek. Gracie Faith chattered the whole way home about the Dawson brothers and how funny Nash was and how Decker let her ride piggyback and that Grandma has yummy cookies and how she was so excited to have her very own piggy. And when she'd exhausted all possible topics, she said, "Mama, I really love Maverick." She hugged herself. "My own baby piggy." Then she sat up. "Can we go back and visit tomorrow? Please?"

"Of course." Even though the thought made her suddenly giddy with excitement, she wondered if she could overstay her welcome at the Dawson ranch. "But maybe we should give the piggies time to be born and get used to their new surroundings before we start staring at them."

She thought about it and then nodded. "Okay."

They pulled up to the house.

Her mother wrapped an arm across her shoulders on the way into the house. "You and Maverick seemed happy."

"We are, I think. We have some things to work through, but it's nice just to be back together."

"I believe it. It's nice for all of us to see you like that."

"When do you start over at the school?" Her dad held the front door open for them.

"I have training for a couple days, and then they want me with the students Monday of next week."

"That's so exciting." Mom hugged her. "Everything is just so nice since you've come back."

"I know. I wonder how long it can last. But then I remember it's always been pretty great here." She kissed her mom and dad and then headed up the stairs with Gracie Faith in tow. "I'll see you both tomorrow."

She was almost all the way up the stairs when her mom called up, "I forgot to tell you. Someone by the name of Daniel called."

Bailey stopped and reached a hand out to the wall to steady herself. "What did you tell him?"

"Nothing. Just that you weren't here. He asked about Gracie, seemed like a nice man."

She shook her head. "Why is he calling me?"

Her mom looked from Gracie to Bailey's face and then nodded. "I don't know, but if you don't want to talk to him, we can always block his calls."

Bailey's breath sounded ragged to her own ears. "I don't know what I want right now." She started walking again. "Except for bed. We both want to lie down on our pillows and go to bed, right, sugarplum?"

"Yes, Mommy. I'm so tired."

"Let's talk about this tomorrow."

"Good night."

She read as many books to Gracie as she could before

falling asleep. She nudged herself awake again. Then she changed, brushed her teeth, and took a good look in the mirror. "You don't need that man back in your life."

Her reflection completely agreed with her. But her mind was conflicted. Could she really keep a father from his child if he wanted to be in her life?

But what about Maverick? She shook her head. What about him? He wasn't ready to make any commitments. She could tell. His trust level was still low. And she didn't blame him. She wasn't sure they could make it work, given what they'd been through. What if Daniel wanted in? What if he wanted to be a real dad? Wouldn't that be better than a family full of uncles—even if one of them was Maverick Dawson?

Her heart said no. Her heart wanted Maverick, wanted what she had with the Dawsons. Daniel had hurt her, had thrown her out when he found out she was pregnant. It was Daniel's fault she had spent years trying to make something of herself all alone; it was Daniel whose promises had gotten her to leave Willow Creek in the first place.

She sat back against the wall at the head of her bed and remembered the day he'd called.

Her wedding dress had been hanging up on her door-frame when her phone rang.

Thinking it was Maverick, she answered, "Do you wanna see the dress before you help me take it off?" She loved to shock him and couldn't wait to hear his laugh in response.

But then a man's voice she had never heard before answered, "That depends on who's asking."

"Wait. Who is this?"

He laughed. "I'm sorry I'm not who you were expecting. If I were to guess, I'd say he is a very lucky man."

Daniel had charmed her and made promises. "I saw your YouTube channel. I watched every video on there, and I hope someone else hasn't snatched you up already. You've got talent."

She'd been astounded to hear his praise of her music.

"You write your own songs?"

"Yes, I do." She'd told him about the next lineup she had on paper and that she was set to sing at the next county fair. She scoffed now, knowing how naïve she'd sounded. She fell right into his greedy trap.

But to give him credit, he had tried to promote her. He'd thought she could make it. He just hadn't had anything lined up like he'd claimed. He had been starting as fresh as she was, a new talent agent scooping up Nashville talent to shop around. Only, first he had had to get her to Nashville.

They'd talked for an hour before he'd asked her to come do an audition.

"Oh, I can't do anything like that until after the wedding."

The quiet on the line lasted so long Bailey thought he'd hung up. "Hello?"

"I thought you understood. This window is only open right now. That's fine if you want to pass, but you'll just have to wait and see if anything like this ever opens up again. It's not every day I find such a perfect fit between producer and talent."

She held her breath and fell into the nearest chair. This was her one big chance flying out the window. "Well, then I'm sorry to say I'll just have to turn you down."

He'd left his number with her in case she changed her mind. And she'd thought it was over. But his offer had festered and nagged at her. It stole her happiness even at the county fair when she sang for a few thousand people, thinking that if she'd gone to Nashville, it could have been twenty or thirty thousand. She hadn't known anything at all about the music industry or how it worked, but somehow, after one tiny offer from a wannabe talent scout, nothing else satisfied.

Except for Maverick. He was everything to her. The sun and the moon and everything in between. He really was. She'd have done whatever he wanted for the rest of her days. And so she told herself she was happy every day.

Until the night before her big day, when Daniel called her again. This time, there was an incredible offer. The producers had been to the county fair and heard her sing. They wanted her. But she had to be in Nashville in five days. Could she come right after getting married?

She wanted to say yes. But she called Maverick first. Before she could say anything about Nashville, he told her he'd been offered a spot on a world championship rodeo team. He was full of energy about how exciting it would be for the two of them to travel. And how'd it feel to be the wife of the world champion?

She hung up the phone that night, promising to meet him at the church the next day.

Only she never did.

She headed to Nashville, and Daniel took her to that producer who he claimed was so interested. Except it turned out to be a cold call. They'd never heard of her before. And neither had any other person he'd tried to set up meetings with.

And by then, she was living with him, and they were a full couple in every way. She was so ashamed, so sorry, and so caught up in his promises of the next big gig, the next opportunity, the next audition, that she kept on. Because if she were successful, then it might justify what she'd done. She'd have something to show for herself. Everyone back home would see she hadn't been running away but chasing her dreams.

And she couldn't face Maverick. The thought of seeing him again after what she did, after living with this other man, after not even telling him she was leaving. It terrified her.

Reliving that awful time of her life felt raw and scary. Some of her old insecurities returned. Daniel was dynamic and charming, and she'd always felt naïve and awkward when he was around.

And now he was calling her parents' house. Of course, he could find the number, but a part of her had hoped he'd forgotten about her or that he wouldn't know where she'd gone. She really hadn't thought he'd ever try to contact her again.

The last night they were together, she had cooked him a really good meal, had dressed as carefully as she could, taking extra time with her hair and makeup. But he'd been distracted. He'd already been coming home smelling like someone else's perfume, so she knew something was going on, but she thought maybe her news would change all that.

"I'm pregnant."

His fork had stopped in midair, and it wasn't out of joy. She remembered his final words before asking her to find somewhere else to live. "I say we terminate the pregnancy.

If you want to go through with it, then you're doing it without my help."

And so she'd left.

In that moment, she thought he'd given up all rights to ever being a part of Gracie's life. But what if he wanted to do right by her as a father?

She pulled her covers up to her chin, rolled over, and tried to block out all other memories, but they flooded through her anyway.

The day she moved out, he hadn't come home from work. So she packed up everything by herself and loaded it into the waiting taxicab. She'd moved to a cheap motel. The first night, she'd curled up in a ball on her bed while the tears drenched her pillow, and she told herself to go home.

She decided she would leave in the morning. It was the only thought that comforted her enough to get her to sleep.

But then morning had come, and she found a new drive to make it on her own. She was gonna prove to Daniel that she didn't need him. She was a talent. And she would find work without him.

Five years later, she found herself back on her parents' front porch with Gracie at her side.

And it was the best decision she'd made since she left.

What did Daniel want? He always wanted something. She tossed and stressed and hated everything about that night, the night when she should have been reliving Maverick's kiss.

Maverick.

She was done with worrying. She pulled out her phone and texted Daniel, *What do you want?*

You still up?

Yes.

I told you. I want to meet our little girl.

She stared at that message until her phone's screen switched off. Then she pressed the button and stared at it again. For most of the night, she studied his response. *I want to meet our little girl.*

But she didn't answer him. Instead she pulled her old Bible off the bookshelf, opened the word pages and started to read.

She didn't tell anyone about Daniel. Not for two more days.

On the day she and Gracie went over to visit the new baby pigs, it was still heavy on her mind. Maverick answered the door almost before she knocked.

"Hey." His smile was warm and genuine, and she fell in love with it all over again.

"Hey."

He grabbed his coat.

"Now, wait a minute, Maverick. I want to see my girls too, you know." His mama came around the corner, her happiness larger than her diminutive frame.

Gracie ran to her, and Bailey smiled to see her daughter enveloped in the warmth of a hug from Mama Dawson. "I'm gonna meet my new baby pig!"

"Oh, I bet that baby is gonna love you."

She giggled.

"When you come back, I'll have warm food and some goodies to take home."

"Thanks!"

Maverick held open the door. "We ready?"

Gracie ran out into the front yard. And Bailey's heart

felt a little lighter. Maverick stopped her as she passed by. "And good morning to you."

She looked up into his face, drawn in as always. His lips hovered close to hers for a moment.

"You look delicious in the morning." His deep voice rumbled through her, his sexy morning scruff making him look almost irresistible. She lifted her chin, and when their lips met, everything felt right again. It was quick, and when he backed away, only a portion of her anxiety returned. Then he winked, and they followed Gracie out toward the barn. His fingers linked with hers, and they swung their arms as they walked.

"So, yesterday was a long day." Maverick grinned and squeezed her hand. "Without you in it."

"I know. I kept looking at my watch, wondering if it was today yet." She laughed. "But I did get a lot of prep work done for my first day at work."

"Those kids are gonna love you."

"I hope so. 'Cause I'm gonna make them work." She couldn't wait to get going next week.

"That's what I like to hear. Work is the Dawson way."

"Your parents sure raised some amazing sons."

He looked out over the rolling hills all around them. "They really did. Even as adults, we all know it means something to be a Dawson. We all know what's expected."

"You gentlemen are a dying breed."

He stood taller. "Mama raised us right."

Bailey laughed. "She certainly did."

They walked through the barn doors, and Gracie was already kneeling down in front of Lulu watching the babies eat. She held her finger to her lips. "I know it looks like they're eating her, but they're just getting their milk."

"That's incredible." Bailey shook her head. This whole scene was surreal and brought her back to the day she'd met her first piglet.

Maverick leaned back against the wall next to the stall. "Now, are you gonna tell me what's bothering you?"

"What?" She stood in front of him. "You still think you can read me?"

He looked away. "Well, obviously not well enough."

She reached for his arm and waited until he looked into her eyes again. "I'm sorry."

He shrugged. "Are you going to tell me?"

She glanced at Gracie, who was still mesmerized by the piglets. "The quick version is…" She took a deep breath. "Daniel, the man who…" She waved at Gracie.

"Yes, I understand."

"He has reached out to me a few times this week. Said he wants to be a part of her life."

He took a step back. "Oh."

"Yeah."

"What did you tell him? What do you want?"

"Nothing, and I don't know. I mean, I know what I don't want. I don't want anything to do with him. I want to run as far and as long as I can so that she doesn't have to have anything to do with him."

"But?"

"But I don't know if that's right. He is her father."

Maverick waited.

"Even though he kicked me out of his life and told me he was disowning her and me."

"Well then, seems to me like he lost his chance. I'll be the first one to tell him what an idiot he was."

"So…what do I do?"

He frowned. "I don't know. "

"That's not helpful."

"Well, how could I? It's not my place to say. All I know about him is that he's a lying cheat, that he has no honor, that he's a coward, that he is utterly selfish..." He ran a hand through his hair.

"But it's not your place to say?" She lifted an eyebrow then shook her head and stepped closer, leaning against his chest. "Sounds like I should stay as far away as possible."

"I think so. But is this me talking for me or for you?" He looked away. "Am I being selfish like he was?"

"You are everything he is not."

He wrapped his arms around her and held her close. Her eyes closed, and she clung to him. She would do anything to be able to keep things as they were. But to keep a father from his child? A daughter from her father? How could that be the right decision?

She didn't know anything for certain. Reading her Bible the other night, she just kept going back to the same verses in Proverbs. "Trust in the Lord with all thine heart..."

Maverick smiled down at her. "We'll figure this out."

A whiff of uncertainty breezed by in her thoughts. Was this really Maverick's problem to deal with? Didn't he have enough to handle? A part of her, the old independent part, thought she should try to own up to her issues and handle it herself.

Chapter 14

Maverick laughed every time he thought of little Gracie staring at the sow feeding her young. He picked up the phone. As soon as Bailey answered, he grinned. "Hey! So I want to talk to you about something."

"Oh yeah, what's that?"

"We're setting up something for the fair."

"The county fair?"

"No, the big ol' fair. The state fair."

"Cool! What do you have going?"

"You and me, on our horses."

Her silence made him smile.

"And you at the microphone, Gracie with her pig, our big Jersey cow, the guys doing a show. It'll be a family event."

She didn't answer.

"Well?"

"Okay, I think I'm in. For everything except me at the mic…or me on a horse."

"That's all the parts that include you."

"Not really, Gracie will be in it."

"Doesn't count for you. She's her own girl."

"Touché."

"Come on. We'll be brilliant."

"Us on a horse. What do you mean? Like our old show?"

"Yes, of course. We'll work on it, beef it up."

"Hmmm. I don't know, Maverick. All joking aside, I haven't done anything like this for forever."

"Perfect. We'll have to practice."

She laughed. "Okay, I can practice, but just 'cause it means being on a horse with you. But I'm not singing."

"Why not?"

"They bring big names to the show. I won't fit in."

"You'll be just right."

"No. Maverick, I already tried all this. I can't make it. I choke."

"Now, that's just not true. I've probably heard you sing more than anybody, and you've never choked, not even once."

She was quiet; the emotion felt thick.

"Except that one time. On the Cheetos."

"Ha. Very funny, Maverick. I just don't think I can do it."

"I'll let you think about it. The Dawson family is going to be a big sponsor this year, and so we get to pick an opener for one of the bands. I'll pick you if you're game."

"Wow, I don't know what to say. If I was brave, I'd jump at this, but I shut the door on that dream a long time ago. I gave up."

"Comin' home doesn't have to be giving up. I say coming home was winning and the dream is still possible."

"Of course, you do."

"Let's talk about it at BJs tonight."

"We going to BJs?"

"If you want to come dancing."

"Okay, I'm in."

He grinned. "See you at eight."

When she hung up, he rested his boots on his desk and leaned back in his chair.

"Things going that well?" Decker leaned his tall frame up against the doorway.

"I sure hope so." He gestured to a chair. "Come on in."

"I have the finances for this quarter. And the tax estimates."

"Did you pass it along to the accountant?"

"I will, but I wanted to let you know we had another loss."

Maverick clenched inside.

"Just thought you should know."

He lowered his boots back to the floor, his irritation swelling. "What do you think we should do about it?" His tone was flat, even.

"I don't know. This ain't my thing…" His voice dwindled as he searched Maverick's face. "Look, Maverick…"

"What, Decker? If this ain't your thing, then whose thing is it?"

Decker glanced at the door like he wanted to run, but Maverick had no mercy. "Decker."

His brother sat, tossed the paperwork onto Maverick's desk, and then crossed his arms. "I get it. Everything got thrown at you when you wanted to be doing other things. But I didn't throw it at you. None of us did."

"Well, now I'm asking you to take up some of the slack. You came in here with a problem and no solution." He lifted the papers and held them out. "Come back when you've figured out what to do about it."

Decker stared at him for a moment and then nodded, respect in his eyes. "Will do, boss." Then he stood, grabbed the papers back, and left.

Maverick pressed his thumb and forefinger against the bridge of his nose. Why was everything suddenly getting to him? He'd been shouldering all of the ranch business for years. Why was he suddenly losing patience now?

The rest of the morning continued more or less the same. He handled ranch business by lashing out at his brothers and handing off responsibility. At their late breakfast, every brother had reason to brush his shoulder and groan and complain at him, which they did.

Their mama entered, ready for lunch, to a room full of grown men not speaking to one another. "What's this?"

Everyone but Maverick turned away. He looked her in the eye. "What's what?"

Nash snorted. "This, Mother, is the result of your eldest son getting after us all morning."

"Just handing out the responsibilities as usual. Seems about par for my day. Except now maybe someone else will actually do their job."

His brothers threw up their hands as they resumed complaining.

Maverick looked around at the bickering, angry faces and cleared his throat. Twice. What a mess. He'd gotten everyone riled up, and he felt a twinge of guilt. He stood up at the head of the table. "Brothers."

They ignored him.

"Brothers!" At last, they quieted down.

Maverick smiled, chagrined. "Maybe I've been a little harsh?"

They turned their eyes to him. He glanced at Mama, who dipped her head for him to continue. He couldn't tell whether she was supportive or unhappy with him.

"I think maybe I've finally...um..."

"Cracked?" Nash lifted a hand in the air.

"Or something. But I would like to talk about this with everyone. Because it's not like this is coming out of nowhere."

Decker nodded. "True."

"But can we keep the overbearing, demanding older brother act to a minimum?" Dylan glared at him. "We're all busy, and we get it. We need to divide up the work better."

"Fair enough." Maverick gestured at the meal in front of them. "Why don't we eat? We can talk over Mama's delicious food."

Mama lifted her glass. "Yes, let us eat. And remember your dear father as we do, the man who loved you all and would be so proud of the honorable men you have become." Her gaze moved over the table to each of the brothers. "Perhaps I'll pray this time." She bowed her head, they held hands. "Dear Lord. Bless my boys. Bless our ranch. May the peace and spirit of unity and love, your Holy Spirit, be with us always. Amen."

They started their meal. Maverick pressed his fork through the pile of whole wheat pancakes on his plate and brought a delicious bite dripping with syrup to his mouth. But even the pancakes felt old, without luster. He lifted his eyes and then lowered his fork. No one else had started eating. They all watched him.

"What? You might not like what I said to you today, but you have to admit I had a point." He eyed them. When no one responded, he pointed his fork toward them. "Decker."

Decker messed with the food on his plate. "You're right. We come to you with the problems, but you shouldn't be the one to solve everything."

Maverick nodded, satisfied.

"But," Decker continued, "none of us knows better than you how to fix this stuff. We're all just guessing here. Dad…he just always knew what he was doing."

Nash folded arms across his chest. "Exactly. And just because it was Dad's dream doesn't mean it's my dream."

The tension in the room rose a notch. But Nash held out his hands in a placating gesture. "I'm all about the Dawson Ranch. But to me, it's more about who's sitting here at this table than it is about what happens out there."

Something inside Maverick knew his brother had a point. "But where does that leave us? Someone's gotta keep things going around here, or we don't have a Dawson Ranch. We don't have a place to live. And…" He choked back a sudden lump in his throat. "And we'd lose the last bit of Dad we have with us."

Mama's eyes teared up, and he hated to see it. She shouldn't be a part of these conversations. Every eye turned to her.

She dabbed her mouth with her napkin. "Boys, no one ever said ranching life was easy." She paused to share a loving gaze with each one of them. "How much we give to the ranch just depends on how much we want out of it."

Maverick nodded.

Nash grunted. "Oh, stop with your nodding, Maverick. I'm so sick and tired of feeling like you're the one who has to take a hit for all of us. Look, if you want to ride, go ride. Just do it. Your decision doesn't mean we all can't ride. If we ride and you don't, it doesn't mean our circuit is stealing yours. Make your own way in the world, man. If that's what you want, do it." Fire flashed in his eyes.

"And then what?" Maverick asked. "You guys gonna make sure things stay afloat around here?"

Decker nodded. "We already talked about this. I think we could work on a way to divide up the responsibilities better. We already said we were willing to trade out circuit years."

"Instead of trying to be like Dad, we could just work out our own way of handling things." Dylan leaned forward. "Like a board of directors." He was the one Maverick had thought would get an advanced degree and leave them all to work in a big city. He'd always had the business sense that most of them lacked.

They relaxed into a more productive conversation, and the brothers started eating. Mama looked relieved. And Maverick felt parts of the ranch responsibility leave his shoulders one piece at a time.

He sat back in his chair. Why had he suddenly snapped?

His phone dinged. *Bailey.* He stood. "I gotta take this."

Nash pointed. "And there's the reason for the new Maverick."

They watched him leave. Was Bailey his problem? He held the phone up to his ear.

"How you looking?" she asked.

When he heard the smile in her voice, he just couldn't think she brought him anything but a new hope for happiness in his life at last. "I need to see you."

"Come over."

And with those words, he realized his loyalties had changed. Without a thought, he grabbed his keys and headed for his truck, lunch with Mama or no.

Chapter 15

Bailey hummed with happy expectation. Maverick was coming over. Then her stomach twisted in knots. *Maverick was coming over.*

Daniel had called again. Bailey ignored it, but after staring at her phone for an hour, she opened up their text conversation. She'd been somewhat disarmed. Her mind had kept her awake with thoughts of how that could be. And now she felt disloyal for harboring any positive feeling for Daniel at all. And yet, he'd been…nice. Not apologetic, but interested. Humbled maybe.

Maybe.

Did she tell Maverick? No. She didn't need to make him aware of every emotional development regarding Daniel. But that left her feeling like she had secrets. And it felt all too similar to those ill-fated weeks leading up to her wedding.

But when she heard his truck pulling up the drive, she pushed her nervous anticipation aside and ran to meet him. He leapt out of the truck so that he could get her door.

"Well, hey! Where we going?"

As he shut the passenger door behind her, a reckless happiness filled her.

By the time he sat beside her in the driver's seat of the truck, she was ready for some serious fun.

He leaned across the middle console, his grin welcoming. "Are we in a hurry?"

She shrugged. "I was until you got here. Now, time can slow to a crawl, and I'll be happy."

"Perfect. So, back to the lake?" His eyes sparkled.

"Or the trestle?"

He nodded. "You're on. But the lake is happening eventually."

"I'm not one to back away from a challenge."

He reached for her hand. "You really aren't. So, about that singing in the fair."

She groaned. "Of course, you'd turn this conversation to my singing at the fair. What would I even sing?"

"Anything. Come on, you're incredible. Sing 'Always and Forever.'"

The song she wrote for him.

He colored slightly. "I like that one."

"I hope so. My heart and soul went into that."

"Well, why not that one? You know it still, right?"

"Of course."

They drove along, his thumb caressing the back of her hand while she considered what he wanted from her. He wanted an act in the fair, but what he really wanted was for her to keep pursuing her dream. And she had so firmly closed the door on it that she wasn't sure her heart could be open to the possibility again.

"Look, Bailey, I just want to hear you sing again. At a microphone, in front of a crowd who appreciates you."

She closed her eyes. "The crowd's always amazing, isn't it?"

"Absolutely. Not quite like our county fair but still real good. They're ready to have a good time."

She had to admit the idea of standing at a microphone in front of a friendly crowd after those years of rejection sounded pretty darn good. "I'll let you know later today." Even if it terrified her, she was really tempted.

They pulled to a stop in front of the large trestle bridge that spanned across the Guadalupe River.

Her heart hummed. "Wow, that thing is high."

"We were crazy as kids."

She eyed him. "You having second thoughts?"

"No way. We're doing this. If only to prove we both still got it."

She closed her truck door and stretched her arms above her head. "I think I might need a little proving."

"Me too."

He grabbed her hand again, and they walked slowly toward the bridge, the thing growing in height with every step.

Then Bailey made her way to the side where a long metal railing started at the ground and lifted in a gradual slope to the top of the bridge. The metal had large bolts at intervals, just large enough to grip with her hands and use as a foot brace as she climbed to the top.

Maverick grunted behind her. "Don't look down."

"No way. Not 'til I'm sitting at the top." She remembered the view was amazing. It was even more awesome when a train raced beneath them, practically touching their dangling feet. But that rarely happened.

She climbed higher.

"I still like this view I've got right now."

She snorted. "You did not just say that."

"Well, why not? I love you in a pair of tight jeans."

Her laugh carried out over the area beneath them. "Unfair timing."

"What? 'Cause you can't retaliate?"

"No, 'cause I can't do anything fun about it."

"Oh, that sounds nice."

She pushed on. They were almost at the top, and inching out over the top of the bridge required concentration.

"Easy now," Maverick cautioned.

"Yeah." The ground seemed so very far away. "Maybe not the best idea."

"We'll be careful. And then maybe not do this again." He laughed. "Our younger selves would be rolling their eyes at us."

"Oh, we'd be shamed." But she had Gracie to think about now, and he had his whole family depending on him.

"How's the ranch and everything?" She eased out over the top on hands and knees, then scooted forward to make room for Maverick behind her.

"Not great."

Shocked at his answer, she maneuvered so that she could turn around to face him.

He carefully straddled the top of the bridge and then let out a long exhale. "That was way scarier than I remembered."

He hadn't yet met her eyes. But she waited. Something was bothering him.

"I'm a mess."

"Maverick, you are not a mess."

"No, I am. All the guys are mad at me, Mama's worried. I keep getting after everyone to do their job. And the ranch is losing money. The guys aren't all in. Until Mama looks at us all with her soft sad eyes and talks about Dad—then everyone bucks up and works harder. I was happy to take over, sort of, but suddenly I'm wanting the guys to pick up more of the slack."

"As they should. Why does it all fall on you?"

"'Cause Dad left it to me."

"But I'm sure he was thinking you would delegate, right? Hand out responsibilities?"

"Probably, but it's different telling my brothers what to do."

"Do they not appreciate it?"

"No, they don't, but it's more than that. All of a sudden, I'm just not satisfied. I used to do most of the work happily, but now I'm wanting them to pitch in extra."

She studied him. Did he wish to go after his dream? Was it finally time for Maverick to ride the circuit?

"Nash thinks I should ride the circuit."

"I think that's a great idea. Why don't you?"

His eyes clouded. "I don't know if that's the solution. I love the ranch, and I love the circuit. But I think what's unsettling my saddle is I've found something I care about more." His gaze lifted to hers, and she sucked in her breath.

"You have?"

"I have. And nothing else matters. Bailey, when you left, my world went flat, meaningless. And then Dad passed away, and I filled my life with duty. I thought I was happy, or at least satisfied, but when I saw you again, everything came back, all the happiness, the purpose, the meaning in my life. I know what I've been missing all this time. And I see that, really, I don't care one lick about any of the rest of it. All I care about is you."

Her heart pounded. She didn't deserve this. And she saw, once again, what she'd done to a good man, the man she loved.

He wasn't finished. "I'd love to work the ranch with you on it. I'd be thrilled to ride the circuit if you're in the stands watching and waiting for me when I'm done. Or better yet, riding the barrels like you used to. But what do either of those things mean to me without you?" He shrugged. "I guess lately I've just realized how little I care about any of it."

She scooted closer, trying to pretend she wasn't hundreds of feet in the air. "Listening to you talk like that makes me sad."

"Sad? That I want to be with you?"

"No, sad that you haven't had everything you deserve in life." And that she'd been the cause of most of his unhappiness.

"Well, what I'm saying is ranch or circuit, your teaching at school or even a new singing career, whatever it is, I want in, Bailey. I want to be a part of your life. Forget the whole friends thing. You said you're not going anywhere. Well, I'm not either."

"Why're you telling me this way up here?"

He looked around. "I don't know. I didn't really plan this, you know."

She swung her legs.

"Why? What's wrong with up here?"

"Well, you remember when we were in high school and you went through that hillbilly accent phase?"

He leaned back and laughed. "Ah. Now, I don't rightly know what you're on about, seeing as how I always talk just the same."

"Well, I was just thinking, with you talking all sincere-like, we needed to be somewhere a bit cozier. Because, like you used to say—"

"Them's make-out words." He laughed again. "I'd forgotten, but you're so right." He scooted closer until their knees met. "I still think we should seal this with a kiss. How about it, Bailey. Will you be my girlfriend? Again?"

She leaned forward and rested her hands on his thighs, knowing she didn't deserve it. But she wasn't able to resist. "Yes, I will."

He met her halfway and pressed his lips to hers. "Much more of that later."

A bright light blared from the darkness, blinding them, and for a minute, Bailey thought the police had finally started enforcing the no-trespassing rule. But then a train whistle blew, and she and Maverick grinned.

"Whooop!" He waved a hand in the air.

It was considered good luck to be there while a train went underneath. They'd only managed it once before—the first time he'd asked her out.

He reached forward and took her hand. Then they grinned as the train vibrated underneath them.

When it had passed, he checked his watch. "You ready to go dancing? I'm full of energy, and I can't even move up here."

"You know I am! Let's go."

He scooted back until he reached the end and then maneuvered to start climbing down the bolts again. She gave him some space and then followed.

As soon as they were on the ground, he pulled her close. "You're shaking."

"I'm not used to this stuff anymore."

"Good. 'Cause I was scared to death up there."

"You were?"

"Absolutely. But I'm glad we did that." He wrapped his arms more tightly around her. "Glad we rode it with a train. And more than anything, I'm glad you said yes." He searched her eyes. "I love you, Bailey."

"I love you too."

He dipped his head and pressed his lips to hers in a desperate sort of familiarity she found difficult to resist. She rose up on her tiptoes and clung to him like she would never let go. He lifted her up and held her in his arms while their mouths moved with a beautiful energy, a oneness they'd always had. He tugged on her bottom lip, drawing it into his mouth. Then he ran his tongue along hers, teasing, asking.

She responded, lifting herself in his arms, pulling herself as close as she could get, and wrapping her legs around his waist.

He held her close, raised his face to meet hers, and kissed her more.

She wanted Maverick. Forever and only Maverick. And she wished this one kiss could wipe away all the wasted years.

His energy more insistent, his kisses coming faster, he walked back toward the bridge and pressed her up against it.

Her feet dropped, but she clung to him until she didn't think she could stand any more. And that's when he slowed and paused, resting his forehead against hers. "Wow, Bailey. There's a lot of years of waiting in that kiss."

She lifted her gaze to his, full of longing. "I reckon I'm just about done waiting. How about you?"

He studied her, his gaze traveling every inch of her face. "I reckon you're right. And I want to do this the right way."

She nodded, expecting nothing less from him.

Then he stepped back and took her hand. "Let's get to BJs so I can show off my pleasantly mussed and well-kissed girlfriend."

She laughed, reaching a hand up to her hair. "Am I…"

"Gorgeous. Just how I like you."

"Then that's all that matters." She stepped in beside him, and they swung their hands back and forth as they made their way to his truck.

When they pulled in front of BJs, the place shook with music. Bailey grinned. "Just like old times!"

"Just like old times."

They hopped out of the truck and ran to the building. They flung open the door and pressed through the crowd to the middle of the dance floor.

The place looked just as it always had. Thick dark wood made up the walls and the furniture, and the tables lined the edges of the room. The place was packed. Bailey glanced around at the faces; most looked familiar, but she couldn't place them all.

Maverick pulled her into his arms, and they danced long into the night, one song after another.

He swung her around in a circle, brought her back into

his arms, and Maverick murmured in her ear, "I've never been happier."

Bailey didn't think her life could be any sweeter.

Maverick dropped her off at home with a long, lingering kiss full of promises. She was so full of courage, of hope, of desire for a happy future that she didn't think anything could disrupt her happiness.

Until Daniel called again that night. And this time, because she was full of courage and confidence, she answered him.

Chapter 16

Maverick picked up a bouquet of daisies and headed to the middle school. He knew it had only been two days since he'd last seen her, but in his mind, that was two days too long. He had a pile of paperwork on his desk and some tough decisions to make on the ranch, but first, he wanted to see his woman. He grinned. Bailey was his woman again. What an awesome thought.

He had already thought about proposing. She seemed as much in love with him as he was her. But the thought brought out a shuddering fear through him, so he'd pushed it off to think about later. Last time, he'd been certain she loved him, and he'd fully expected a beautiful bride to walk down the aisle toward him. But she hadn't.

Would she do it again? Nothing was certain, ever. And at least for now, he had a willing, fun Bailey. He didn't want to risk changing things.

He stopped by the front office. "Hey, Peggy." The woman sitting at the front desk was a friend of theirs from high school.

"Oh, she's gonna love those." Peggy leaned forward, almost pouring herself onto the table between them. The girl's starry eyes made him smile and step back toward the door. "You just take those right on in. Do you know where she is?"

He shook his head. "The choir room, right?"

She gave him directions, and he scooted out of there as quickly as he could. As he walked through the halls, he considered his fears. He had good reason to be afraid she would walk out again. He'd been so blindsided the first time, he had no reason to think it wouldn't happen again. Except that it couldn't. Bailey would never do that a second time. Would she?

He rounded the corner and stopped in front of the choir room door. He could hear the kids singing. So he peeked in, careful not to let Bailey see him. She stood at the front, waving her arms at them like he'd seen all conductors do. She was leaning in, her face intent, her smile genuine, and the kids watched her, their eyes shining with hope. Maverick grinned. She loved this, and the kids loved her.

Then she stopped them. "That was beautiful. So good, in fact, that I want to give you something special to try. Only the really good singers can handle it, but I think you guys can do it no problem." Even Maverick was intrigued. She sang, and her whole face transformed. While she was enjoying leading the kids, she was full of joy when she sang. Her heart seemed to fill her song. She swayed for a minute and then stopped. "Did you see what I did there? Who can tell me?"

The kids raised their hands, and she continued as if nothing out of the ordinary had happened, but Maverick felt changed. He knew singing was her passion. Using her voice in the way she just had made Bailey who she was. But she'd been beaten down enough to give it up. She'd put her daughter first and worked so that they could survive.

But her voice was part of what made Bailey who she was. He'd like to pound some sense into that man Daniel for more reasons than one. And into his past self. He was grateful to realize now what he hadn't seen when they were younger. They needed to focus on her dreams as well as his.

The class worked on repeating what she had done. After a minute of mediocre attempts, she told them to take a break. And as she turned to walk back to her desk, he smiled through the window at her.

She stepped back in surprise, and Maverick was gratified to see just how happy she was to see him. She rushed to the door, flung it open, glanced over her shoulder, and then stepped out into the hall. "Maverick, hi."

"Hi yourself." He held up the flowers. "I just wanted to drop these by."

She took them from him. "My favorite." But her eyes held questions.

"Really I just wanted to see you."

Her grin melted him further. "Good, 'cause I wasn't gonna survive another day without seeing you."

"Come over after work. Let's ride."

Her eyes lit. "Oh, I'd love that. Can I bring Gracie?"

"Gracie is always welcome. I want to see her almost as much as I want to see you. Besides, I have some tricks I want her to work on with her pig."

"Has she named it yet? She won't tell me."

"I don't know. For now, she calls it Pig."

The students were getting restless, so she stepped back toward the door.

But Maverick pulled her closer. When their faces were kissably close, he murmured, "I love you." Then he pressed his lips to hers, their softness making him only want her more. "See you soon."

She swayed, dazed for a minute, and then smiled a soft, sleepy smile. "See you soon."

"Who was that?" Maverick heard as he walked back down the hallway, satisfied for a moment that he'd seen her.

His mind moved to the paperwork for the ranch. As he pulled up to the house and made his way into his office, he thought about the losses and the stress on all the brothers, and he wasn't sure what he would do about any of it. If the ranch became no one's priority and everyone's chore, then it wasn't what his dad had meant for them.

A stack of mail waited. His books and financials waited. Decker had written up a plan to bring in some more money that he needed to look at. And his own pending decisions waited.

One letter sat on top, from a real estate developer. He suspected he knew what it said. They got these all the time, people hoping to buy pieces of the property and build them out. But he'd tossed every other letter in the trash. Not only did he not want to sell his father's land, he didn't want the ranch to be surrounded by new developments.

But he opened this one, wondering if it was time to start at least considering it. As he glanced through the proposal, he was happy to see they would subdivide into larger acreage plots with nicer homes. He felt better about that than a set of stores, a strip mall, or high-density housing.

He set the letter aside. Then he pulled out a letter from their accountant. The details were way more discouraging than he'd thought. He reached for Decker's report, then he groaned. His brother had known the numbers were this bad, knew it was gonna take more than a few simple fixes to change things. He'd come to tell him last week not because he was just being lazy, but because this problem was larger than what he could handle alone. And Maverick had thrown it back in his brother's face.

He picked up his phone. When Decker answered, Maverick said, "Hey, I'm sorry."

"What for?"

"I'm just now looking at the numbers, really looking, and you were right to come to me. This is a bigger issue than I realized."

"Yeah, but you needed to preen your feathers for a minute before you realized it."

"Very funny. I looked through your suggestions. They're good."

"But…"

"I don't know. It might not be enough. Maybe we should talk about selling some land."

"Hay just isn't a viable income for the land. Maybe we plant enough for our own livestock, but that's it."

"And up the cattle. We could earn more doing cattle."

"But not as much as we could if we sell the land."

The quiet on the other end brought the corners of his mouth down. He hated to say it, but they should consider all their options. What would be a viable income for their mother? How much could she manage? Or how much would Maverick want to continue with his own family, with…he almost didn't dare think their names…with Bailey and Gracie?

Finally, Decker said, "We should bring it up to everyone."

"Do you think we should?"

"You're afraid they're all gonna want to sell."

"Yeah."

"Maybe ask Mama first."

His mother stood in the doorway.

"And here she is. Okay, Deck, thank you. Talk to you soon."

Mama held a plate of food and a tall glass of lemonade.

"Hmm. Did you make all that for me?"

"I sure did." She entered the room and placed it on the tiny corner of his desk without piles of papers.

He shifted things around and moved his lunch right in front of him.

"Talk to me, Maverick."

He took a bite of his sandwich. "Mmm. You make the best sandwiches."

She waited, love in her eyes. "Every woman should know how to reach a man's heart. I'll give Bailey the recipe."

His gaze lifted, and he dared to ask what concerned him most. "Do you think she'll stick around this time?" The next bite went down slowly, rubbing his throat the whole way.

She sighed. "I think so. But I thought so last time too."

He nodded and gazed out the window. "I keep telling myself to be careful, to watch myself, but she already had my heart even before she came back. There was nothing I could do about it."

She patted his hand. "Then we'll just all hope she is more careful with it this go-round." She watched him eat for a few more minutes then said, "But that's not the only thing weighing on you, is it?"

He shook his head. "Decker and I don't know what to do about our financial situation."

"Tell me."

He hated to burden her, but he knew she was his father's closest business partner as well as his wife. So he told her how they were losing money, more every year, how the Dawson cows weren't getting picked up for premium prices as much anymore, and how they lost money on their hay crops.

"Have you considered leasing more of the land?"

"Or selling it."

The pain that crossed her face was brief, but it was enough for him to clench his fists.

"We should bring up the solutions to everyone and see if they can think of anything else." She stood. "I'm sorry you bear so much on your own."

He shrugged. "Despite what I was acting like the other day, I really can handle it. I just don't always like my solutions."

She nodded. "You know, the best thing for our Dawson Ranch was when you were out riding and winning championships. That's what brought our name to the national stage."

He raised his eyebrows. "Really?"

"Absolutely. You boys doing really well on the circuit did a lot to help sell cows."

He toyed with his pencil. "Do you think Nash can pull off a win?"

"I can't be sure, but certainly nothing like you could do. I know Decker will likely win again, though, and that will help."

"And our sponsorship of the state fair. Our show. That will help."

"I think so." She turned to walk through the door. "Bring it up to everyone in a nice voice, and we'll see if we can come up with a plan."

His mouth lifted at the corner. "A nice voice. Have I been that terrible to live with?"

"I think you're just finally noticing that you put yourself on hold all this time."

"Probably."

Her eyes looked tired, but her face was full of years of happiness.

"You doing okay, Mama?"

"I'm just fine. What mother wouldn't be with a family of men like I've raised?"

He nodded, and she left him to ponder his thoughts, which were now much more hopeful. Even if they had to make changes, or sell some land, he felt like everything was gonna work out.

He worked through all the other, less challenging decisions and then checked his watch. Bailey and Gracie would be coming soon.

He walked back through the house toward the kitchen. His mama's signature chocolate chip cookies were obviously in the oven. "Mmm. Mama, what's the occasion?"

"My granddaughter is coming over, that's what." She smiled, and he warmed at the thought.

"She's such a good little girl. Bailey has done a great job so far."

"She really has. But you know, Gracie Faith acts just like her. I remember when our Bailey was little."

Maverick nodded. "I don't remember her that little. But that just goes to show parenting is all about example."

"And love and trust." His mama moved around the kitchen. "Even though you don't see it, you're just like your father."

He warmed in happy disbelief. His good mama could praise him all day, and even if he didn't believe her, she still made him feel better. "What are you doing in here?"

"Well, I've got the cookies cooking, but then I got to thinking she might want some soup. It's chilly out there. And then I knew she'd want a grilled cheese sandwich, because what child doesn't want that with their soup?"

He moved toward her, arms out. "You're the best grandma in the world, just like you've always been the best mama."

She accepted his hug, squeezing him back with a fierceness he had come to appreciate. "Now, I've got to hurry. Unless you want to help, step over there so I can get my work done."

He laughed. "I'd be happy to help."

Then a little girl's voice shouted through the house, "Grandma! Grandma!"

They both laughed.

Gracie came running into the kitchen. "It smells so good in here!" She looked around until she found the plate of cookies. "Ooohhh."

"Would you like one?"

"Yes!"

Then Bailey entered the room, and Maverick's world felt whole again. He pulled her into his arms. "Mama and I were just talking about what a good girl Gracie Faith is."

They watched her savor the hot, melty chocolate chip cookie.

Bailey smiled, and the pride was evident in her eyes. "You are a good girl, aren't you, Gracie?"

She nodded. "Mm-hmm." She stepped up to Mama Dawson and placed her hand inside the welcoming reach of her grandmother.

"Would you like to come see the flowers I planted?"

"Yes!" She squealed, and the two headed out back.

Maverick leaned back against the kitchen counter and pulled Bailey to him. "This is what I've been missing since I last saw you."

She leaned into him and wrapped her arms around his middle. "Me too." She lifted her chin, and he immediately captured her lips with his own. Hungry for more of her, he kissed away as much of that hunger as he could, but her eager response only made him want her more.

Lingering as long as he dared with his mother and Gracie right around the corner, he kissed her once more and then tugged her hand. "Let's get you on a horse."

"I can't believe we're going to do this again."

"You can't mess with genius. The crowd's gonna love it."

"I'm gonna love it. I think. If I don't fall off."

He pulled her close and wrapped an arm across her shoulder. "I'll catch you. You've got me, Bailey."

As her smaller arm hugged him around the waist, he knew it was true.

Chapter 17

After Bailey and Maverick rode for a solid hour to much clapping and cheering from Gracie and Mama, he hopped off his horse and ran to her daughter. "And now, Gracie Faith. Are you ready to work with your little piggy?"

"Yes!" she shouted, jumping up and down.

Bailey loved them together. "I'll take care of the horses in just a minute. I want to ride a little longer."

Maverick's eyes met hers. A thrill rushed through her at their intensity. "You know I love you best up there. And singing...and with Gracie Faith."

She laughed. "Anywhere else?"

He shrugged. "Probably."

Then he hopped over the fence before he reached for Gracie. The two of them headed for the barn. Bailey rode over by Mama Dawson. "Thank you for being her grandma. She really loves you."

"I think she was meant to be ours all along."

Bailey tried to swallow her tears. "I think so too."

They shared a moment together where Bailey wanted

to apologize all over again for ever leaving such a beautiful family.

But then Mama said, "I know you had to leave. You got something inside you that wants to sing and share your voice. I saw it every time you sang."

"But I should have said something."

"That you should. Just like you should do so now, if you got something to share." Her eyes saw more than Bailey thought she was revealing. And then thoughts of Daniel crowded her mind, thoughts she'd been pushing away. She nodded, suddenly uncomfortable, and nudged her horse to take her out into the wider paddock area. Maybe if she ran fast enough, the ghosts of her past would leave her alone.

She pushed the horse out to the farthest corner of the small field. And then she stopped, turning in a slow circle so she could see all the land around her. Beautiful. The land filled her in much the same way her singing did. She loved this ranch like she did her own.

She realized, as she drank in everything, she'd do a lot to protect it. She was a Dawson as much in her heart as she hoped to be in her life. Did she want to marry Maverick? Could she finally take that step? Of course, she could. She'd already told him she wasn't going anywhere. She'd do anything to be his wife.

Her phone rang, and without thinking, she answered it. "Hey, love. I'll be over there in a second."

The quiet on the other end concerned her. "Hello? Maverick?"

"So you're back with Maverick?"

"Daniel."

"I'm glad you at least took my call even if you didn't know it was me." The self-deprecating tone made her smile.

"Well, you can't blame me. He's pretty special."

"So you've said. Does he know how awesome you are? 'Cause I wish I'd known sooner."

She sucked in a breath. "Do you?"

"Yeah, I was a jerk. Look, I don't want to come between you and Maverick. Again. But I was thinking maybe I can come out there to meet my daughter."

"She's not your daughter."

"What are you saying? I'm pretty sure she is."

"Let's just be super clear. You said you wanted nothing to do with her, that if I was gonna keep her, she wasn't your responsibility."

"I know what I said. But I feel differently now. She's something special, I bet, and I just want to meet her. I won't even get up in your life. Can I meet her as, like, a family friend or something?"

She groaned. "In. Out. Done. Don't plan on staying more than an afternoon."

"Okay. I will." The breathless hope in his voice made her wince.

"And, Daniel. There is no us. And you're not her dad."

"Got it. And thanks. This means a lot."

"Mmm. Don't make me regret it." She hung up the phone. All the peace and happiness of the Dawson ranch was gone, replaced by a worrisome anxiety she couldn't shake.

She rode to Maverick's horse and reached for its bridle, and then led both horses over to the barn.

As she took off their saddles and brushed them down, she couldn't shake the cold heaviness in her heart. Surely letting Gracie's father meet her had to be the right choice? As she poured some alfalfa into each of the horse's bins, she just couldn't convince herself to be happy about Daniel coming. She wanted to wrap her arms around Gracie and run away, far and fast.

As she made her way back across the empty paddock and headed for the pig barn, she knew she was dragging her boots, but she didn't know what to do about it. Maverick would know right away something was bothering her, but she didn't want to tell him and especially not his mother.

Gracie pushed open the barn door and came running to her. "Mama!" She leapt into her arms. "Guess what!"

"What! Tell me!" Her heart started to feel lighter, and she managed a real smile for her daughter.

"I'm gonna name my pig Nash!"

She laughed. "What!"

"Yeah, Maverick said that was a good idea. It's 'cause Nash helped me pick out the right one. And we're gonna win, so I want his name up there with me."

"That's a great idea!" She laughed again and looked for Maverick.

He stood leaning in the barn's doorway. "I had very little to do with it."

"That I can't hardly believe." Bailey lowered Gracie to the ground. "Why don't you show me what your Nash can do."

Gracie ran back and picked up her piglet. "He's so smart." She took him to a larger, empty stall and tied a mini rope bridle around the pig's neck.

"How does she know how to do that?"

"She's a natural. I promise. Just explained it once."

"Wow." She paid closer attention as Gracie worked with her pig. At first, the animal was reluctant, resisted instructions, but Gracie kept at it, kept asking, kept showing, and soon, Nash the pig was prancing around doing what he was told. "You're so good at that, love." Her eyes flitted to Maverick's. "And I'm sure you had a great teacher."

Maverick was everything a young girl should have in a father. Again, the guilt piled on as Bailey considered the consequences of her choices. Maverick could have been her father.

He sidled up to her. "I love your little girl, you know." His eyes were full of sincerity, full of love. "All this time, I've been thinking about our kids, wondering what they would have been like." He dipped his head toward Gracie. "She's so much more amazing than I even thought."

Bailey's eyes filled with tears. "If only you were her father."

Hurt flashed through his face. "Understood." He stepped back and called out, "Well done, Gracie. Should we give little Nash a bath?"

"Wait. No, you don't understand."

"What don't I understand?" He turned around, his face closed, his eyes guarded.

"I'm just..." She glanced at Gracie, who was paying closer attention. "I was just saying I was stupid."

Gracie widened her mouth in surprise. "Did you just say a bad word?"

"No, what I meant was dumb."

Gracie's expression did not change.

"I made a poor choice."

She nodded her acceptance and then turned back to Nash the pig.

Maverick's expression became less guarded as he looked from mother to daughter.

"What I'm trying to say, Maverick, is that if I'd been smarter, you would be a father already. And we wouldn't even be having this awkward conversation."

"And I'm just sitting here noticing that I still could be, because I love you and her, and you're pushing me out." The hurt grew in his eyes, and he turned away with a forced cheerfulness. "You know, piglets don't like baths too much, but I once read if you bathe them in milk, it makes all the difference."

Gracie took his hand and glanced back at Bailey. "Are you and Mama okay?"

"Yeah, we're great."

Gracie frowned. "Whose daddy are you? Why's she mad about it?"

"I don't know, Gracie Faith. Some things are just too confusing for me to figure out. But one thing I do know, you are one special girl, and I'm glad we're friends."

"Friends." She frowned. "I thought we were family."

Maverick turned to Bailey. "That's right. We are." Then he scooped her up in his arms and kissed the top of her head as they rounded the corner to the hoses.

"Do you want to be *my* daddy, sometime?" The tentative manner in which she asked broke Bailey's heart.

Gracie held her breath.

"I'll be your daddy any time you want. Just call me Daddy, and we're good to go. But no matter what you call me, I want you to know I'm here for you. I love you, Gracie Faith."

She nodded and then wrapped her small arms around his neck. "I love you, too." He squeezed her tight and led her back to the pig barn.

Once Nash the pig was washed and dried and back with his mother, they sent Gracie inside with Grandma.

Maverick came to join Bailey at the split-rail fence. He didn't say anything, but Bailey found his presence comforting even though they were at odds. She pointed up to the ridge which formed the property line between their ranches. "You know I love this land?"

He faced her, but she didn't turn. She gestured all around them. "I love all of it. It's special."

His boot dug around in the dirt at their feet. "You look good here."

She nodded. "I feel good here. I think I would do anything for your papa, for the Dawson land." She needed to talk to him about Daniel, especially after that beautiful talk he had with Gracie. If he was wanting to be in her life, be her daddy, then what was she doing letting Daniel come? Why did there even need to be a Daniel? Did she have any sort of obligation to Gracie's biological father? She ached to tell Maverick, desperately needed his advice. But she didn't want him to feel obligated or responsible for them.

He rested his head on his hands. "We're in some trouble, financially."

"What? What kind of trouble?" Her mind started spinning.

"The kind where we're talking selling off pieces." He looked up at the ridge but didn't say anything about it being one of the pieces in question.

She followed his gaze and shook her head. "No. You can't do that."

"Bailey, we might not have a choice."

"No, you always have a choice. You can't sell off parts

of the Dawson Ranch. There has to be another way. Have you guys talked about this?"

"A bit. We're gonna have a meeting this week. I gotta make some tough decisions."

"Well, I say no. No way. Think of your mama. Think of the town. Your brothers…"

"What about me, Bailey?"

She quieted. The only thing she loved more than the land were the people in her life. Maverick. Gracie. "What do you want?"

"What do you mean?"

"What do you really want? When you say think about you, what does that mean?"

He looked away. "I don't know."

"The circuit? You still want to ride?"

"Yeah, well, no. I liked it. I told you. I want to ride if you're there."

She nodded. "I'll be there. If that's what you want." A sick feeling rose inside. "Does that mean we have to give up the ranch?"

"No, just a piece or two, maybe. Whether I ride or not, we might have to do that." He turned to her. "Mama says if I ride, the name recognition might help the ranch. People will buy our cattle. I could be my own sponsor."

Bailey nodded, but a sad feeling filled her. "Then do it."

"What? Just like that?"

"Yeah, do it. Go ride. Get on this next rodeo circuit. They'd take you."

"What about you?"

"What about me?"

"You've got your class at school. Gracie. You're not coming on the road right now, I'd imagine."

She breathed in and out twice before she answered. "You need to go without me."

"That doesn't make any sense."

"It does to me. And you're right, I can't leave right now. But you can. And I'll be here. I'm not going anywhere while you're gone. We'll come watch when we can."

He shook his head. "Just like that."

"What do you mean?"

"You can send me away like it means nothing to you? What about you're not going anywhere? What about that?"

"Look, what do you want from me? I'll do anything. You want me to follow you on your circuit, to leave everything and bring my daughter on the road? I will if you want."

He searched her face. Then he shook his head. "I guess not. Not if you're not excited about it."

She didn't know what else to say. He wanted to ride. She knew it. And she wasn't gonna take it away from him. She wasn't gonna be the reason he stayed behind and gave up his dream. Especially if it was gonna save the ranch. She was trying out a little bit of that trust she'd read in the Bible. This could go in God's hands. It would work out.

"You've got to, Maverick. Follow your dream. Save the ranch. Go do what you've always wanted, and I'll help around here."

"You, what?"

"Sure, I will come be with your mama and fill in where I can." He shook his head like he was gonna turn down her offer, but she saw a flicker of relief pass across his face, and that was enough for her. "Go." She just hoped she'd survive without him and that he really would come back. She'd seen firsthand what the race to success could do to a person.

"I'll be right here when you get back."

As he looked up at the sky deep in thought, she noticed he didn't promise to *come* back. He probably just didn't think of it.

Chapter 18

All night, Maverick turned the options around in his brain. He'd have to talk to the brothers about selling. But maybe they wouldn't have to sell. Maybe if they all did something for the ranch, it would be enough to keep it intact. The fair would help, he knew, but...

He read through the circuit offer again. His mother and Bailey and his brothers all thought he should go. At first, he had thought they were just being supportive of his dream, feeling bad he'd given it up. But now he wondered if they were right, that there was some wisdom in it. If it wasn't just a selfish desire of his own, he could see himself trying to make it work. He could talk up Dawson Ranch everywhere he went, find some sponsors even for the ranch itself. He'd definitely make some connections and hopefully sell a lot of beef cattle in the process.

He'd just about talked himself into giving the guy a call and accepting a position on the team when he wanted to touch base with Bailey about it again. He didn't know what more they could talk about. But seeing her again suddenly became so urgent he left everything unfinished on his desk, hopped in his truck, and hurried to her house.

He turned down her driveway to find a strange car in front. Maybe one of the neighbors had bought a new one. But an Audi? It just wasn't the normal Willow Creek car. It had out-of-towner written all over it. He pulled to a stop under their large live oak. As he stepped out of the truck, he could hear Gracie laughing and playing in the backyard. He smiled. Then his heart clenched. He'd miss that girl. Leaving for nine months of the year with only a few breaks would be hard on him. She'd grow. She'd start kindergarten. She'd learn things. She'd probably be jumping ponies if her grandpa had anything to do with it. And Maverick would miss it all.

Should he consider her needs before his own? Before the ranch's? She was the most important person in his and Bailey's life. He hadn't ever been a father, hadn't ever cared for a child like this. And they weren't married—Bailey had made it clear enough he wasn't the girl's father. But he couldn't help the direction of his heart.

Going over things in his mind again, he realized how much he needed Bailey to help him make this decision.

As he rounded the house toward the backyard, he stopped and moved behind the huge flowering bushes. Gracie was laughing and squealing and then took a great running leap into a man's arms. A man Maverick had never seen before. "Are you my uncle too?"

He strained his ears.

"Not quite your uncle." He laughed. "But I want to be important to you, perhaps even family."

Alarm reverberated through him. *Daniel.*

"Daniel, come inside for some lemonade," Bailey called

from the back porch. Maverick couldn't see her, but her voice sounded light, carefree.

Bailey hadn't said anything about Daniel coming into town. And yet here he was, and things were looking cozy.

But Maverick was having none of it. Bailey couldn't go through with it. If she was even thinking about letting that slug of a human back into her or Gracie's life, Maverick would have words with her. He stomped back around to the front yard and up the steps. He lifted his hand to knock just as Bailey walked by. Her eyes widened. She looked behind her and then hurried to the door. She stepped out onto the front porch and closed the big wooden door behind her.

"Trying to hide something?" Maverick's voice sounded as suspicious as he felt.

She frowned and put her hands on her hips. "So you saw him."

"Of course."

"Well, now's not a good time to just show up, you must know that."

"I think it's a perfect time. Someone's gotta show you the difference between a real man and that lying weasel of a human." She could not actually be considering involving Daniel in her life.

"And you think that's gonna solve something?"

"Well, yeah."

"He's her father."

The hurt he felt at her words cut him super close, but he shook his head. "No, he's not."

She sighed. "Don't you think I feel the same way? Don't you think I know what's going on in your head? But I couldn't tell him not to see her. Could you have?"

He thought of a whole stream of things he could tell

this guy while his fist connected with his face. But as he saw the pain in Bailey's expression, he knew he had to take a different stance. "So this is what you want?"

She nodded. But when he turned away, she said, "Wait, what do you mean 'what I want?'"

Fear barreled through him. He couldn't compete with Daniel, not for something so precious, not when he'd already lost once to the creep. "No, I hear you. I wish you guys every happiness trying to figure all this out." He made up his mind. He was out. Bailey needed time to figure out the whole Daniel thing, and Maverick already knew he was not a good addition to that party.

"Wait, no. Where are you going?"

"I came to tell you I'm leaving tomorrow. To get ready to ride the circuit. Coach wants me practicing, getting in shape, getting to know the guys."

Bailey nodded, her face cold and unreadable.

"So, bye."

"Just like that?"

He nodded and indicated what she had in the house. "Just like that."

She watched him get into his truck and pull away. When he checked his mirror before turning down the road, she was still on the porch.

His phone dinged. Bailey. *What about the fair?*

I'll be back for the fair.

Then he tossed his phone onto the seat beside him. Leaving made him sick. But if he left, maybe Bailey could figure her whole mess out. If he left, he could help Dawson Ranch. Everyone seemed to think it best that he leave, even Nash. And Bailey basically told him he's not welcome while she's trying to figure out

Daniel's place in their lives. Everyone wanted him to go.

So he did. He went home, packed his duffel, grabbed his rodeo gear, put his horse in the trailer, and took off for Mesquite, where he'd hole up and work out to get ready for the circuit.

He sent a text off to his brothers to let them know he was leaving. *We can work things out long distance. Everyone do what we talked about last week. And listen to Mama. We gotta find ways to earn more money for the ranch.*

Nobody answered yet. None of them were big texters. But they'd check in later, and he'd hear what they thought then.

Driving away from Dawson Ranch felt bittersweet. But it was nice to let the problems rest for a time. Was it hard to leave when he knew his heart resided in those hills? So hard.

He didn't know if he could actually get on the freeway going east. But he did. And he survived.

Bailey sent a text. *You really going?*

Yep.

We'll come watch as many as we can.

He responded with a thumbs-up. He'd wanted to say something snarky about them bringing Daniel. But that would have been just straight-up wrong. So instead of saying something stupid, he just sent the emoji. It might have seemed cold or too vague, but that's all he had right now.

Was he overreacting about Bailey having Daniel over? Probably. But it bothered him that she hadn't told him about it. It scared him like nothing else ever had. Daniel had some kind of sick power over her, some dangling carrot of success that Maverick couldn't match. In the past, Daniel had offered adventure, a singing career. And Maverick had offered roots and loyalty. She'd gone with adventure. And now Daniel was sweeping back in with a tie as strong as blood. He gripped the steering wheel. Oh, how he wished Gracie were his daughter.

But he wasn't gonna wait around while Bailey ran off with Daniel again. And he wasn't gonna watch while a man who didn't deserve a second of that young girl's time weaseled his way into her life.

What did Daniel want with them? Maverick just couldn't believe that a man who had treated them both so callously for years could suddenly have a change of heart.

He hoped Bailey would come to her senses. Even if Maverick wasn't around to remind her of what they had together.

It was late at night when he arrived in Mesquite. His truck pulled into the training arena where he'd work with the team before the circuit started. His old boss, Jeremiah, was there to meet him.

He hopped out of the truck, and Jeremiah clapped him on the back. "Does this mean you're in?"

"I'm in."

His grin warmed Maverick. "Let's get Thunder situated and have a talk."

"Is there a trailer for me?"

"You know it. Right next to mine."

Maverick nodded. If he didn't think about what he was leaving, this new adventure could really get him excited.

BAILEY COULDN'T BELIEVE Maverick had just left. She had told him to go, but Willow Creek without Maverick was something she'd never experienced before. As she got ready to head into work the next morning, she dreaded leaving the house.

Daniel had decided to stay for two days, so he was still there. Bailey didn't want to leave Gracie with him alone. Something didn't sit well with her when it came to Daniel. He said all the right things. He seemed like a good and changed man, but she couldn't shake her unease. So she'd put Gracie in her parents' care. "Don't leave her alone with Daniel."

The concern in their eyes told her what she asked was not a simple task. But they nodded, determined.

"When is he leaving?" Her mama made no secret of the fact that she did not approve of Daniel.

"Tomorrow. First thing."

Mama nodded.

Bailey headed off to work after a quick kiss from Gracie. Her daughter whispered, "I miss Maverick."

"I know, sweetheart."

"Who's gonna help me with Nash?"

"We'll figure it out. I could help you, you know. I used to show pigs myself."

"You did?"

"Yeah, I totally won a ribbon one year."

"Okay, then you'll do." Her serious pout was part amusing, part tragic.

Bailey missed him too, like she would a hand or an arm or her ability to sing. What did any of it mean without Maverick? She kissed her little girl goodbye again and then walked out the front door.

Daniel met her on the porch. "Hey, can we talk for a sec?"

She checked her watch. "Yeah, but I gotta get to work."

"Okay, we can finish up when you get home. It's just… have you considered letting Gracie have her dream?"

"What are you talking about?"

"You're keeping her from it, Bailey. It's like you're afraid she'll make it big."

She narrowed her eyes.

"She's a natural performer. You saw her on that sheep, with her pig, she's a pro. Do we know if she can sing?"

This was the Daniel she remembered. The pushing, grasping, talent-hoarding, manipulative man who'd pretended to help Bailey try to make it big.

"That's not the life I want for her, Daniel."

He shook his head. "But is that the life she wants for herself? Don't you think you should give her every chance now so she will be ready if she chooses to follow that dream later?"

"No, I don't. I've lived it. You've lived it. You think I want that life for Gracie?"

"But she's a natural. You had to struggle so much. Your voice just didn't measure up. Your performance…we've talked about this. We know why things didn't pan out for you. But Gracie! She could do it. She's got everything you didn't."

"What are you even talking about?" Her heart clenched in memory of all her failures, of the times Daniel had talked her into giving up. When he convinced her that all her auditions and all her failures added up to one thing: proof she didn't have what it takes.

"I'm just saying you're holding her back. And as her father—"

"Hey, hold on. You are not her father."

"We've been through this."

"I know, and somehow you're not getting it. You gave up your rights as her father when you wanted her dead. You're only what I say you can be. And right now, that's not her father."

He shrugged. "But we could make something of her. She could be huge. It's the break I've been waiting for."

Bailey felt her fear rising. "No." All of the pressure, the promises, the hints of fame, and then the disappointment and the failures came crashing back around her. "No. And if that's what you want here, you can just leave."

"You're kicking me out of my own kid's life?"

"You kicked me and her out when it mattered. I'm just helping you stay out."

"If that's the way you want it."

"That's the way I want it. Stay one more day 'cause she is expecting to show you her pig and pony and all of that. But then I want you gone. And I don't want you to come back." She couldn't bear letting the poison he'd spread in her heart spread to Gracie's. She was precious just the way she was, whether or not anyone ever wanted to sign a deal with her.

His eyes darkened, and for a moment, she was afraid, but then he nodded and turned to walk back into the house.

Gracie's happy squeals only heightened Bailey's worry. At least her parents were going to stay at her side the whole day.

Chapter 19

Bailey didn't call at all the first day Maverick was gone, or the second, or any day after that. He turned off his phone most of the time to avoid checking for her number. Days turned into weeks. Maverick worked hard to get back to what he once was. The coach had him doing his two best events. The bull riding, of course, and the bronc. Which reminded him of Bailey. All of it reminded him of Bailey.

He had survived two weeks without any news from her. He hadn't asked, and she hadn't offered. This wasn't what he'd imagined when he'd left. He'd never imagined Bailey would stay behind. He hadn't assumed she'd be welcoming visits from her ex-boyfriend, nor had he planned to leave on bad terms with the only woman he had ever loved.

He climbed down onto the back of their meanest bull, wrapped his hand around the ropes, and then nodded at the staff to open the door.

Maybe the Old Iron Scare would shake the misery out of him. As he clung to the animal, his brain rattling in his skull, he knew that nothing could rid him of this misery, nothing except himself. When he picked himself up out of the mud, he waved off any help or further training for the day and went to find his horse.

Sitting astride Thunder brought things into perspective. He looked at what he knew. He wasn't happy, but he *was* helping the ranch. He already had two additional buyers for his beef cattle.

He missed Bailey. But she didn't appear to miss him. He would likely beat his own record this year. And he didn't even care.

As he took off over the miles of pastureland next to their practice arena, Thunder raced with a freedom Maverick could never feel. Maverick knew that what he thought would help him deal with his problems had only delayed his having to face them. But he had to see this through. He'd finish out the circuit, win his medals, earn more visibility for his ranch, and then possibly hand the lot of it over to Decker. He seemed the most inclined, perhaps the most interested.

The state fair was this weekend. He would be leaving for home any minute. And he wasn't sure how he felt about seeing everyone. He wanted to see Bailey like he needed air to breathe, but he didn't think he could handle her disinterested eyes or seeing Gracie with Daniel again. He didn't want to be home if Bailey wasn't part of it. He'd done that already.

But he had to go back. Like his dad said, he'd put on his boots, wear his best buckle, and face the worst life had to give with the nod of his hat.

When he rode back to the trailers, Jeremiah was there to meet him. "You headed to the fair?"

"Sure am. I'll be announcing my circuit and team of course."

Jeremiah waved his hand as though it didn't matter. "Are you gonna go see your woman?"

"I don't know if I have a woman. But she'll be there."

"Are you gonna make things right?" His no-nonsense frown gave Maverick pause.

"Well now, sometimes the man's not the one who decides these things."

Jeremiah shook his head. "That's where you're wrong. Plain and simple. It's always the man who needs to make these things happen. If things aren't right, can you think up a few things you could do to make them better?"

When expressed like that, Maverick felt some guilt tug at him. "Yes sir."

"And do you think that doing even just those few things will help her know how you feel?"

"Yes sir."

He nodded as though enough had been said.

And Maverick knew he was right. No matter what Bailey needed to do or not do, he, Maverick, had a long list of things he could do better. Maybe the fair was just the place to start doing them.

As long as Daniel wasn't there.

He wasn't going to marry the woman until the issues with Daniel were settled. If he was going to be involved in this duo, or possibly trio, he felt like he should have some sort of voice in it. And he wasn't sure how happy he was about marrying into a trio that included Daniel.

But marriage or no, Maverick could make sure he didn't contribute to the problem. And as he reviewed his behavior and thoughts, he knew he could improve.

The drive felt long, even though it was only about an hour to the fairgrounds from Mesquite. As he drove into Fair Park's living grounds for the fair participants, he made his way to the Dawson Ranch group of trailers. He knew they were to be housed in the northwest corner of the fairgrounds and that everyone from his town would be near each other. He could house his horses and all his livestock in the stockyards or in their arena. He'd keep his horse with him in the horse trailer, but the cows, the pigs, and the other horses could all go in their own separate stalls in the barns.

He pulled closer. There was a fire already going at one spot, with a group of people gathered round. They were laughing. Someone had a guitar out. The closer he drove, the more familiar the group became until he recognized Decker and Dylan, Nash, and his mother. Gracie Faith came running around another trailer, and he held his breath until Bailey joined her, laughing and creating a stream of bubbles out behind her as she ran. She dipped a bubble wand again and waved it through the air. He watched, a sort of wistful desire clenching his stomach. So far, Daniel was nowhere to be seen.

He pulled in the rest of the way, the crunch of the gravel announcing his arrival.

Almost everyone in the group smiled, Gracie Faith's being the sweetest of all. But Bailey's face went blank.

He hopped out of his car. Gracie ran to him, and he laughed then swung her up into the air. "And how's my most favorite pig charmer?"

"So good! And Nash is the most obedient pig ever."

Nash snorted. And Maverick couldn't help his own enjoyment. "I love the sound of that."

"We are gonna win first prize! We washed him in milk and everything."

"It's Mama's secret recipe for the most perfect pig bath." Maverick grinned at Mama. "How are you?"

"Just fine. But it's so good to see you, son."

"You too." He looked at Decker. "Brothers."

"Maverick." Nash grinned. The others nodded.

Then he turned to Bailey. She looked away, and Gracie ran to her. "Look, Mama! Maverick came back!"

"I see, honey. Thank you."

Maverick's boots moved in a steady path to stand in front of Bailey. "Hey."

"Hey." She glanced at him and then looked away again.

"I was wondering if we could run through our show tomorrow?"

"Sure."

He turned to the others. "You all ready for the Dawson Ranch showcase?"

"Yes sir," Nash answered for all of them. "We convinced Bailey to barrel race too."

"Did you now?" Maverick raised his eyebrows.

She shrugged. "Yes, I thought it only fair that I do my part."

He nodded. And then he didn't know what to say. She looked away. And in their whole on-again, off-again history, things had never felt more awkward.

Bailey shifted. "Hey, look, I'm gonna go get some sleep."

"Oh, okay. I guess I'll see you tomorrow."

"We better practice early."

"I'll come by at first light."

She nodded. "Good night. Come on, Gracie. Time for bed."

As soon as she was out of sight, he joined his family at the fire.

"Well, that was the dumbest apology I've ever heard." Nash dug a stick into the fire.

"Who said I was apologizing?"

"Weren't you? I thought for sure that's what you would be doing." Nash glanced up, his eyes serious.

"Oh yeah? And just what do you think I should be apologizing for? For leaving? I was under the impression that she wanted me to leave."

"For not speaking to her or us for all this time. For leaving on such a negative note. For not trusting her or appreciating the fact that she's there for you."

Maverick narrowed his eyes. "Sounds to me like someone has feelings he didn't have when I left?"

"Oh, stop. No feelings you need to be worrying about." Mama patted the chair next to her. "Come and sit, Maverick."

He joined her. "What's wrong with everybody?"

"Oh, nothing's wrong with them." She looked into the fire.

Nash snorted.

"I just didn't think there was anything to say. I left, and she was mad. She never tried to call me, and so I figured she was making her own happy way with Daniel and didn't need me in her life." There, he'd given his most convincing excuse, but it sounded weak even to his own ears.

"And do you wonder where Daniel is now?"

"A little." Maverick hated that he wanted to know.

"Not here." Mama smiled. "And that's all that matters.

She threw him out. He pressured her to let him represent Gracie as a talent, and finally she just had to say no. He was unhappy, said some things, and she threw him out of her life."

Maverick nodded. "Good for her."

"But she could have used a friend, a support, the man she loves."

"That would have been helpful to know."

Nash snorted. "You would have known if you were in her life at all."

"I don't expect you to understand."

Nash shook his head. "From what I see, I understand much more than you at this point."

Maverick sat back and crossed his arms. "I don't know what you're talking about." Then he stood up. "And you know what? If I can't sit at the fire with my family at the state fair and have an enjoyable conversation, I guess I'll just hit the sack too."

"We'll see you tomorrow, dear." Mama reached for his hand and gave it a gentle squeeze. He'd been dismissed.

"Well, all right. Good night." He made his way over to his trailer. As he walked by Thunder, he clucked. "Easy, boy. Let's have a good sleep, shall we?"

Then he opened up the door to his own sleeping quarters, fell in his bed, and lay awake for hours.

Chapter 20

Bailey had known Maverick was coming. She knew he would arrive any minute. All day, she'd been watching the stream of trucks pulling into the fairgrounds, preparing herself for the moment he would hop out of his truck and his blue eyes would capture hers. But nothing had prepared her for the jolt of familiarity, the desire, or the irrational urge to throw her arms around him and kiss away whatever was keeping them apart.

She had been frozen to the spot when he finally arrived. And then she'd been filled with such a poignant longing and desperate worry that she didn't trust herself to speak. So she ran and hid. And now she lay in bed in her trailer, Gracie's soft breathing giving her a measure of comfort, agonizing over Maverick.

Not a single phone call, no texts, nothing from him these past two weeks to give her any clue how he was feeling. Was he done putting up with her mess? Had she pushed him too far? She couldn't lie in bed any longer. She crept out, tied a robe around herself, slipped on her flip-flops, and opened her trailer door.

The warm air cocooned her, and the night insects hummed a lullaby, but nothing could calm her brain's frantic attempt to make sense of her relationship with Maverick.

Perhaps she should have called to let him know about Daniel. But what would she have said beyond what he already knew? She was just trying to do what was right for Gracie. She'd never dealt with any of this before and had no idea about the ethics or moral responsibility she had toward the man who'd fathered her daughter. Even though he hadn't wanted Gracie, did that mean he didn't deserve to see his daughter? It was complicated. She knew that.

When she realized his incredibly selfish motives, he'd left easily enough. As soon as Bailey had told him he needed to leave and that she wanted nothing more to do with him, he'd been down their driveway before she could even feel guilty.

She had a knot in her gut that told her she wasn't quite through with Daniel yet. But that would be something she worried about when the time came.

So, what to do about Maverick. After the fair, he would be gone for many months still. And that would be fine if they were speaking. But she couldn't stand this silent distance between them. She at least needed to be on good terms with the man she loved most in all the world. Even if he didn't want to pursue anything more than friendship after all, she couldn't bear if he hated her.

She leaned back in her camping chair, scooting down so she could rest her head on the back of the chair. Tomorrow.

She would summon her courage and talk to him tomorrow, at first light, when he said he'd come get her for their practice.

With that thought, she drifted off.

In the haze of sleep, the weight of a soft blanket warmed her chilled skin. Then the feel of lips on her forehead. "Good morning, babe."

She smiled. Maverick. Mmm. But morning fog cleared, and she sat up with a jolt. *Not Maverick.* Her blurry vision made out Daniel sitting next to her in another camp chair.

She leaned back into her chair, pulling the blanket up closer around herself. "What are you doing here, Daniel?" What time was it?

"I heard you were opening for the Honky Tonk, and I came to hear you sing."

Her eyes narrowed. But he seemed relaxed and open. Perhaps he was making a gesture. She closed her eyes.

"You could have made it in Nashville."

She shook her head. "I'm done talking about this."

"It was my fault."

She opened her eyes. For years, it had always been *her* fault. "What do you mean?"

"I didn't know the first thing about being an agent. I didn't know any of the big players. It was all a lie. I tried to make my career with a new talent, with you. But I didn't know what I was doing. I burned bridges, and you suffered because of it."

Did she believe him?

"It's true. I see you believing all the lies I've thrown at you all these years. But you weren't the problem. I blamed you, but it was me."

"I don't see how it matters now, but thank you for telling me."

"You could still make it big. Opening for Honky Tonk is a big deal…"

"Stop." Bailey waved her hand at him. "Just stop."

He held up his hands. "Okay. But if you change your mind, I'm in a better place now, I could try to represent you."

She shook her head, anger rising. "You did not just say that."

"I did, but you obviously aren't in the mood to hear——"

"No, I'm not. I'm gonna say this one more time. Get out of my life."

"Whoa. Maybe you just need your coffee…"

"Well, isn't this cozy?" Maverick stepped into their conversation. "Sleep well?" His eyes were unreadable.

"Not really." Bailey leaned back in her chair again, wishing to sink into the earth.

Daniel stood. "I was just leaving."

"I think that's a good idea," Bailey and Maverick both said together.

She eyed him, choosing not to be amused. Maverick looked guarded, suspicious, resigned. Three things she never wanted him to be when it came to their relationship.

As soon as Daniel made his way out of their campground, Bailey stood. "You ready?"

"Yeah, you?" His gaze traveled from her flip-flops to what must be a messy knot in her hair.

"Not quite. Wanna come in?" She opened her trailer door, and he followed her inside. "Gracie is——"

"Good morning, Uncle Maverick."

His face softened, and his mouth lifted in his signature grin. "Well now, how's my favorite girl?"

She wrapped a trailing quilt tighter around herself. "Great! I'm really excited about the fair. And as soon as Mommy's done practicing, I'm gonna go see Nash, my pig, and then we're gonna go pet every horse."

Maverick chuckled. "The fair's the best, isn't it?"

She puckered her lips and then shook her head. "Nope. Willow Creek's the best. My grandmas' houses, my ponies, even Nash is there too." She shrugged. "But I love the fair."

Bailey's eyes welled with tears. She avoided looking at Maverick, grabbed her toothbrush, and slipped inside the tiny bathroom.

"Me too. Let's talk about your pig."

Bailey could only hear muffled bits of their animated conversation while she tried to make herself presentable. Daniel's presence at the fair made her nervous. He was obviously not finished with them or his designs for their stardom, whether hers or Gracie's. His mercenary goals knew no bounds. To him, people were dispensable when he no longer had a need for them.

She drew comfort from the Dawson Ranch. Surrounded by the Dawson brothers including Maverick, her parents, and Mama Dawson, she felt pretty safe. As long as she was careful, Daniel would soon be on his way back to Nashville.

Once her hair was in a ponytail and she was wearing her riding gear, she and Maverick dropped Gracie off at Bailey's parents' trailer and went to grab Thunder and the horse she would ride.

The quiet between them wasn't uncomfortable, which she found surprising. At last, he said, "I love Gracie Faith."

Her heart clenched with a joyful sadness. "I know. I think she loves you too. It kinda hurts me to hear her say, 'Uncle Maverick.'"

"Yeah. Me too."

A sliver of hope grew. Could he want more, still? "How have you been?"

He shook his head. "I don't know. I'm riding well. I could break my record this year."

"I knew you would."

They started easy with general topics. Things were comfortable, but she felt a great deal of restraint from the both of them.

As soon as their horses were ready, they rode them out to a back pasture where they could ride alone.

"Let's warm up." Maverick started a slow canter around the outside of the arena, and she followed. After a few laps, she fell into the delicious muscle memory of their routine. She let the strength of the horse fill her, and she stretched and balanced and moved. Then as their routine was wrapping up, she prepared for the finale, standing up on the back of her horse while it raced around the arena. Maverick came up beside her and turned around backward in his saddle. They locked eyes for a moment, his gaze beckoning, full of love. Then he nodded, and she leapt through the air, reaching for his raised hands. He caught her around the middle, her legs stretched out behind, and they rode, Bailey flying, her smile large, her eyes closed, until Maverick's horse slowed. He lowered her to his lap, and she straddled him as they rode one more lap around the arena. It's what they had always done—their routine. At this point, the crowd was usually roaring and on their feet.

Maverick held her as they circled, and she felt their

unity. A great surge of oneness swirled around her. She couldn't think of how to describe this incredible feeling that they belonged together.

The horse slowed to a walk and then stopped. But they didn't move. Maverick adjusted his hands on her hips, and with a new confidence, a new softness around his eyes, he said, "We can do this."

She wasn't sure if he meant the routine or them being together as a couple. So she said, "We can do anything."

He nodded and then tucked her hair behind her ear. "I was hurt, so I left. I shouldn't have ghosted you."

"I'm sorry you were hurt. I didn't know what to do, what to say. I'm not good at all of these hard things…but Daniel…"

He groaned. "I don't want to talk about that creep."

"Hear me out. I told Daniel to leave us alone."

The new hope in his eyes warmed her. "You did?"

"Yes. Twice now. I don't know how much he'll listen. He's still convinced I can make it big, or Gracie."

"Is that what you want?"

She looked away. "I don't think so. But this morning, he said it was his fault I didn't make it in Nashville. He actually took the blame for the failures. I feel stronger knowing that. So, now I wonder." She shook her head. "I might always wonder."

He closed his eyes. "I understand."

She didn't think he did. But she didn't think she did, either. No matter what, if Maverick needed her, she wasn't going anywhere. She'd made a promise, and even if he was pushing her away, she was still here for him, forever.

"I've been doing some other things while you were gone."

"What's that?"

"Praying." She felt shy about it, but she wanted him to know.

"I'm happy to hear it."

"I feel much better about some of this mess I created. You're right. I don't have to bear this alone."

He pressed his lips to her forehead. "No. You don't. I'm glad you're praying Bailey."

"And reading. I'm learning to trust that things will work out."

"Maybe I should be doing some more of that."

"Or at least calling me."

He nodded and then clucked, and the horse started walking.

His eyes danced with amusement. "Remember this?" The sway of the horse beneath them rocked them closer together.

She laughed. "I remember."

They circled again, and Maverick pulled her closer. She smiled and enjoyed the energy of their faces close, their mouths ready. His lips were soft and strong. His morning scruff lined his jaw. She eased closer, almost capturing his mouth, and waited. He tipped his head, his lashes lowering. When his lips met hers, she leaned into him. The scruff on his chin tickling her face, his mouth soft, insistent, making love to her in the purest sense. His rhythm matched the horse as they swayed together.

One kiss after another, he spoke to her core. She clung to him, answering with all the love in her heart until she didn't know where he stopped and she began, until the world seemed to be made for only the two of them.

When they paused, he said only, "I love you."

"I love you too."

Were they gonna be okay? Bailey didn't know. But one thing she would always know was that Maverick held her heart. He would forever.

Chapter 21

Later that night the campfire crackled, the embers flaring every time someone blew them back to life. Maverick dug through his foil dinner with a plastic fork. "Mama, these get better every year." He placed a soft piece of stew meat into his mouth. "Mmm."

"Thank you, son. You know it's your dad's recipe."

"Is it a recipe, though?" Nash laughed. "From what I remember, he tossed a bit of everything in the foil and told us to roll the edges and throw it in the cooler."

"Sounds like a recipe to me." Dylan took another bite of his. "Works every time."

Gracie Faith held a long stick with a hot dog on the end, waving in and out of the flames.

Maverick scooted forward and crouched down beside her. "Let's see if we can get some of those flames to actually cook your dog."

He guided her hand closer to the embers at the bottom.

"It's too hot." She hid behind him, her small hand

resting on his shoulder as the other one stretched out the long stick toward the flames.

"Is that better?" He couldn't describe the feeling that came over him as he protected her from the fire, but he knew right then he'd do anything for this little munchkin. "Do you want me to do it for you? You can watch from behind me."

She nodded against his back.

"Happy to oblige, little lady." He tipped his hat.

She giggled. "You're funny."

"Why thank you, ma'am."

Bailey caught his eye, and he winked. Then he made a big fuss about cooking the perfect hot dog. "You see now, you can't have any of the skin looking black or dark. I like the ends to be slightly disformed." He brought the hot dog closer. "You see? Like that." Her hot dog dripped with the juices that had escaped their home. "In fact, where's your bun? I think your dinner might be ready."

Bailey handed her a bun, and she held it open for Maverick.

"There you go. One fully cooked hot dog."

She ran the few steps back to Bailey. "Look!"

"Isn't it yummy!"

Maverick sat in the camping chair next to Bailey and watched their cozy group with great satisfaction. The twins were deep in conversation about something. Nash was making a fuss over Mama.

Gracie climbed up into his lap. "Can I sit here?"

"You sure can, pumpkin."

She curled up into him. "You call me lots of names."

"That's true, isn't it? What do you want me to call you?"

"Whatever." She yawned. "I can tell you really, really like me."

His grin spread across his face, almost hurting his cheeks. He turned to Bailey. "Did you hear that?"

"I sure did."

"That's incredible." He rested his cheek on the top of her head for a moment. "I'll tell you a secret your mama can know too."

"What?"

"I do really, really like you."

She smiled; he could feel the movement against his chest. Then she closed her eyes.

Mama came over with the guitar. "Last night, Bailey sang for us. And it was the best part of the whole day." She held it out for her.

Bailey glanced at Maverick and then took the guitar.

"I'd love to hear you sing." Maverick didn't think the night could get any better.

"What should I sing?"

"Sing the happy song." Gracie's little voice surprised him. He'd thought she was asleep.

"That sounds like just the song."

Bailey strummed the strings. "The happy song it is."

Her words were whimsical and fun, and the tune was catchy. Soon they were all singing it on repeat until Nash waved his hands. "Okay, all right. I'm happy already."

Gracie giggled.

Then Bailey played a few notes, adjusted the tuning, and started singing a song he'd never heard before.

"You and me. Swimming in the creek. Climbing up the apple tree and swinging on the gate. You and me. Together."

She went on to sing of all the things they'd done together. It started when they were young, then she sang about their high school antics, even the trestle bridge. His heart started pounding as she got closer to their wedding day. "I said I do, but can I do what he needs me to?" She sang of expectations and hopes on the horizon and then ended with "and I always love him so." Repeated over and over.

Her eyes were shining when she finished. Maverick wanted to pull her into his arms right there.

Then Nash called out, "It's just a little bit awkward."

Everyone turned to look at him.

"Yeah sure, 'cause you know, Bailey's singing songs about me. With Maverick right there…"

They laughed, and it broke the seriousness of the moment.

"What are you gonna sing at the show tomorrow?" Maverick toyed with her ponytail.

"Do you wanna hear that?"

"I know I do." Mama wrapped a blanket around her shoulders even though the night air was warm.

Then Bailey broke out a fun, fast-paced honky-tonk song. Everyone was clapping, and the twins got up and danced in a circle. She entertained them for another hour, and Maverick loved hearing the sound of her voice again.

Her face was shining, and he could see what he'd only noticed now that they were older. Singing filled her with life. Something about using her voice like this made Bailey more who she was. And he loved to see it. A part of him promised that one day he'd help her reach her dream.

The next morning, they all got dressed in their rodeo costumes. Maverick wore his signature champion outfit from their county rodeo. Bailey wore her costume from her barrel racing days. Even Gracie Faith had a new costume. It looked the same as Bailey's but with a bright pink star.

She was thrilled, twirling around in her little skirt over and over. Her little boots had matching pink stars. Her hat was trimmed in pink. And Nash the pig had a bright pink bow. "They're gonna take off the bow before we show him though. It's not allowed." She stood up straight and tall, and Maverick couldn't be prouder.

"Now, you're ready?" he asked.

"I'm ready."

He nodded. "Good girl. Your group is first, you know."

They made their way to the Dawson Ranch box seats. Everyone around them was buzzing with excitement.

Maverick heard Bailey ask Dylan, "Do you think anyone will come?"

"Oh, they'll come. If only just to see him." Dylan pointed at Maverick.

Maverick was happy he'd been practicing. As the arena filled up, he knew he was gonna need to rely on some of that practice.

The emcee announced the clowns from Willow Creek and then their sponsors.

Maverick stood and led Gracie down the stairs. "You're on in just a minute."

He laughed at the bounce in her step, and as they passed a group of boys, he held back his grin at her little nose that went up in the air. She looked back over her shoulder to see if they were still watching. They were, and her cheeks blushed red.

"Now, Gracie. We need to be concentrating."

She went to Nash the pig's stall and called to him. He

came prancing over like he was born to follow her every wish.

"You're gonna blow this whole thing outta the water, little darling."

"Nash is such a smart pig. Thank you for teaching me, Maverick."

"You're welcome. Now get out there and show them what you and Nash can do."

The announcer began the Willow Creek 4-H program introductions, and Maverick and Gracie Faith moved over to the entrance, joining the other young people in their group. Maverick grinned like any father would, watching Gracie do all of the required tasks with exactness. When it was her turn to walk Nash in front of the judges, she was careful to nod and smile at them like he told her to. She paused longer than the others before her turns, and she was in all respects the absolute best kid out there.

The crowd went crazy when they were done, and the announcer explained what the 4-H program was and what these kids did. "And now the judges are tallying their scores. We will announce the winners in just a moment…we have it, folks. We have our winners." Grace held his hand, the tightness of her grip telling Maverick just how much she wanted to win.

He couldn't blame her.

He held his breath as third place and second place were announced.

"And now, for the winner of the gold medal. Gracie Faith Hempstead from Dawson Ranch!"

The crowd went crazy. He could hear his brothers and Bailey in the stands. Gracie jumped up and down and squeezed him around the leg. "I can't believe it!"

"The contestants can come get their prize ribbons at the ribbon desk. For the first-place winners, we'll have a ribbon ceremony at the end of the show."

Their group went crazy again at that announcement. And Gracie and Maverick high-fived each other. Then he said, "That's a lot of love you got up there."

"And down here too." She put her small hand in his, and he suddenly knew what it meant to feel like a king. He stood taller and led her back to their seats.

She received a rousing welcome back in their box. And then the show continued with one event after another. Dylan went out and roped calves, but then Decker beat him. The audience loved that. Then the barrel racers were up.

"Why aren't you out there?" Maverick jerked his thumb toward the women flying across the arena, circling barrels and then running back the other direction. "You literally slay at this."

She laughed. "I didn't have time to get ready. When I added up all the people, we had enough. So I stepped out of this one."

"Wait, have you been planning this event?" Maverick looked from her to his mama and back.

"Of course, she has. And doing all the other stuff too, mind you." Mama jabbed him in the arm.

"What other stuff?" He turned to Bailey.

"Oh, you know, you left your ledgers and task lists, so I've just been going down the items, making sure the important stuff gets finished."

Maverick was astounded. "You have?"

"Sure. I told you I'd help out with what needed to be done."

"That you did. Well, now I need to be thanking you for that."

Mama humphed. "You certainly do. This pretty lady might very well save our ranch."

The whole time he thought she was ignoring him, she'd been holding things together for him while he was gone.

Bailey held up a finger. "Before you get grumpy at your brothers, just know I told them what to do and not do, and so they were just following orders."

"She's worse than you." Nash groaned. "In a good way."

The announcer asked for a drumroll. "I think this might be our cue." He winked at Bailey.

She stood up. "Oh! Oh, you're right."

They raced down to the lower levels. Their horses pranced and whinnied when they saw them as if they knew they were up.

Maverick walked beside Bailey, and suddenly, again, all seemed right in the world. "Let's shock and amaze."

"You know it."

They swung up onto their horses and rode out together through the opening and into the middle of the arena.

The crowd went crazy when they announced the reigning world champion. And they even went crazy when the announcer shouted Bailey's name. The two stopped in the center, and then their music started. And they forgot everything but each other.

Once they finished their number, and then Maverick went out on his bull and beat his world record time by a quarter second, they closed out the show, and everyone made their way to their next activities. But the Dawson family stayed put.

When they were finally more or less alone, Mama patted Maverick's arm. "Now, you looked good riding the bull. Real good."

"Thank you, Mama."

"But not nearly as good as when you rode with Bailey. You two are meant to be together. Can y'all just figure that out?"

"Amen." Nash shook his head. "It's obvious to everyone but you. Apparently."

Maverick just grinned. "Oh, believe me. It's obvious to us too." He reached for Bailey's hand. "And did anyone see this little angel, Gracie, on the winner's blocks?"

"Oh, we certainly did," Mama said. "Your second win, but your first blue ribbon, child. What are you gonna do with it?"

She tapped her chin. "I think I'll hang it on my bed."

Maverick whooped. "Now, did you know that's just what your mom used to do with hers?"

"And just how are you knowing what she put on her bed, young man?"

"Seriously, Mama? They've been friends since before beds were a big deal." Nash shook his head.

Bailey just grinned, and so Maverick went with it. He tapped his watch. "We best be moving over to the big stage."

"You're right." Bailey stood. "Can you hang on to Gracie for me?"

He lifted Gracie's hand wrapped in his own. "You got it."

Bailey hopped on her toes. "I'm suddenly so nervous."

"Don't you worry about a thing. Just pretend you're sitting with us around the fire."

"Yeah, or singing to me in the bath." Gracie nodded. "You're gonna do great, Mom."

She took two deep breaths before she left them, running toward the backstage doors.

Maverick put Gracie up on his shoulders. The whole family grabbed their sponsorship seats up near the front. Maverick moved with anxious energy. He wanted her to love performing. He wanted the crowd to love her. But when Bailey walked out onto the stage, wearing a long, sparkly dress, Maverick's mouth went dry. She was outstanding. In his mind, she looked better than any star he'd ever seen on any stage. The whistles around him started up, and every man in the place called out to her. It made him want to start throwing punches.

"Unclamp your mouth, brother. They're just appreci-ating your woman." Nash rested a hand on his shoulder.

"I think they best appreciate her in another way." Maverick wanted to join her onstage and stare down any man who thought she was anything other than a beautiful singer.

The music started, and the guitar and drums were loud enough that everyone quieted down. The crowd started dancing and jumping in their seats, and then Bailey began to sing.

Maverick was mesmerized.

"Whooo!" Decker called out. "She's amazing."

Maverick nodded, his eyes glued to the stage. He held Gracie in his arms, and the two of them watched her and no one else.

The music slowed down, and Bailey swayed and belted out a ballad that brought people to tears. Then she had them rocking out again to a faster number. She was incredible in every way.

By the time she was finished and the headliner was about to get ready, the lead singer came out and joined her at the microphone. "You're really something. Why don't you stay and join us?"

"What do you say, Texas? Should I join these guys?"

The crowd responded with deafening cheers. And so she joined them. She filled in on harmony and danced and sang backup for the rest of the night.

When at last the show was over, and Gracie was asleep against his shoulder, his brothers and Mama went back to their campsite while Maverick waited for what seemed like a long time backstage.

Just when he was about to ask someone if she'd gone out a different door, she came walking by with three men, one of them Daniel.

Fear shuddered through him. Here it was. The moment she decided to leave. Again.

As they approached, he heard Daniel say, "Excellent. We'll draw up the paperwork and get this going. Thank you, gentlemen." He shook each of their hands. "We couldn't be more excited to get going." He draped an arm around Bailey's shoulders.

Then Bailey shook their hands, and the small group walked around a corner. No one had even seen Maverick leaning up against the far wall.

Chapter 22

Bailey hoped someone would still be awake when she finally made it back to their campsite. The main manager at Glowstone, Theo, had driven her back himself. They'd finally gotten rid of Daniel, and she was able to tell the manager a bit of their history. "He's not my agent." She hoped Theo would still want to work with her.

"Oh good. I'd much rather work with someone we know." He'd given her a list of agents.

As she hopped out of Theo's car and thanked him again for his interest, she thought she might fall over on the spot. Her body was exhausted, but her mind was going a hundred miles an hour.

Had she just been offered the dream she'd chased for all those years? Right here in Texas? The irony of her life never ceased to amaze her. She fingered Theo's business card and then stuck it in her back pocket. No one need know anything about the offer just yet.

She was looking forward to unwinding in front of the fire with the gang and talking through their amazing day.

She wanted to see Maverick, maybe sit on his lap and feel his arms wrap around her in a solid and comforting way. But when she walked up, everyone had already gone to bed. Even the fire had gone cold.

"I must be really late."

She headed to her trailer. As she lifted the handle and quietly opened the door, she imagined how it would be to finally come home to a warm bed with Maverick in it. How she could wake up in his arms and they might raise more children together. After so many long years of loneliness, she longed to marry Maverick like she never had before. He hadn't mentioned it yet, not really. Would he ever ask her again? Rebuilding trust took time, she knew.

The door shut behind her, louder than she meant it to, but Gracie didn't even move. Poor kid had to be super exhausted. She smiled, thinking of her on Maverick's shoulders at the concert. Nothing could have made her any happier than to see Maverick out there cheering and her little girl shouting with just as much energy from on top of his shoulders.

She took off her bracelet and noticed an envelope on the table. Her name was written on the front in Maverick's handwriting. Her heart clenched, and she knew she was about to read bad news.

She tore it open and scanned the page, her hands shaking.

Dear Bailey,

Congratulations on your new record deal. I feel lucky I saw your group right after the deal went down. (I think that's what was going on anyway.) You looked so happy. Daniel seemed in a good position to step in as your agent, finally. I wish you the very best while you go out and grab this dream. It's been a stubborn one, but now's your moment. I guess we both get to live our dreams.

I noticed today a couple areas where I'm weak, so I'm on my way to Mesquite to continue training. Let's talk more this time while we're apart. Might make it easier...though I don't think anything can ease the empty hole I feel when we aren't together.

All the same, I love you! Go get your dream. You are incredible. I would never want to take this from you.

Maverick

She held the letter to her chest. He was the best of men, the very best.

The chair scooped her up as she fell into it. What was she to do? Maverick was off living his dream and wouldn't be home for the next nine months. Did she head out to California to start recording?

———

MAVERICK WON in all of his events during his first rodeo back on the circuit. He swept the winner's blocks. Everyone chanted his name. The next rodeo, the same thing happened. And the next.

He was back in Texas, doing the Fort Worth Stampede, hoping that this would finally be the night where he beat his record at an official event. The rodeo was televised. He wanted everyone back home to see it. He knew his brothers were busy with ranch stuff, and he hadn't heard from Bailey in a few days. So he didn't know if anyone would be in the stands. He doubted they would be, with the local fair going strong and the cattle needing to be bought at auction.

Bailey still hadn't given him the details for her contract

or when she would head out to California. And since a part of him didn't want to know, he hadn't asked much.

This rodeo moved in much the same way as all the others. Maverick told himself he wanted this life, told himself he wanted to ride. But the more he did it, the more he realized he was bored. He'd told Bailey before—none of this meant anything to him without her in it.

But being here was helping the ranch. And he did want that record. His competitive spirit was burning as bright as ever. Even though he was competing with his own record, he wanted to beat it. Wanted an excuse for being gone. He paused. Bailey had said almost the same thing about her situation when she'd been in Nashville. She hadn't wanted to come home until she proved to herself it had all been worth it. And now he finally understood.

But he also remembered what he'd thought from an outside perspective. If he wasn't happy chasing this dream anymore, couldn't he just call it quits and go home?

His bull riding event was up next. He climbed up on the fencing around the chute. Then he lowered himself onto his bull. Hopefully this guy would get good and bothered and want to tear a hole in him so he could win those points.

A voice called, "You got this, Maverick!"

Bailey! He lifted his head, searching the crowd for her face. She waved, and he smiled. Exhilaration filled him. She was there to see his ride. When he was done, he could pull her close, kiss her senseless, and then do it again.

And now he had a record to win with his woman watching.

With hands gripping the loops, he nodded to his team. He nodded to his team. The chute opened, and his bull tore out into the arena, as mad as he'd ever seen a bull. He kicked, and dug, and twisted in the air, trying to get Maverick off his back. But the seconds passed, and Maverick stuck to him. At the buzzer, he slipped down and ran for the opposite side, toward the chute—toward Bailey.

Normally he'd have run to the side, climbed the wall, and sat up out of the bull's reach while he waited for his scores. But Maverick suspected he'd done something big just now, and he wanted to experience it with Bailey.

The shouts from behind came a second before he felt a powerful impact at his back. He was flung forward into the dirt, and the world went black.

MAVERICK'S EYES OPENED, but they felt heavy and full of sand. He reached his hands up to rub them when he heard someone gasp.

"Maverick?"

A hand squeezed his. He tried to turn his head, but he couldn't. He tried to speak, but the words came out in thick monosyllables. His breathing picked up. What was wrong with him?

Then her face came into view, Bailey's smiling green eyes filled with tears. "Welcome back, cowboy."

"Have I been gone?" The words he meant to say came out all garbled and foreign to his ears, but she answered.

"You've been unconscious. But just for a day."

A throat cleared. It sounded like Nash.

"Okay, maybe two days. But not very long."

He tried to nod, but his head felt trapped.

"You're in a brace 'cause they're worried about your neck."

And now he wanted to know exactly what had happened. He tried to move, to sit, to turn his head, nothing.

"Hey, hey, settle down. I'll explain."

He blinked furiously.

"Oh, that's good," Bailey said. "We could communicate this way. Blink twice if you want me to tell you what's going on."

He blinked twice and then scowled.

"Hey, he's still got his sense of humor."

He grunted.

"Or maybe not."

If Bailey was smiling and making jokes, it couldn't be as bad as he feared.

"You are not paralyzed."

He let out all his air in relief.

"You are simply in a suspension. Your head and neck are held absolutely still, but your legs move. See, try to wiggle your toes."

He did, and the movement brought him an absurd amount of joy.

"You will be out of this contraption any minute, and then we can see how your neck and head are."

He blinked ten times.

"Okay, so you came running across the arena, away from the bull, which of course triggered his rage. That guy tore after you like I've never seen. He lifted his legs and kicked you straight in the back. It was so fast, no one could stop him, not even with the tranquilizers." She grimaced. "So you went down and hit your head at a weird angle. They were worried you'd broken your neck when you didn't stand back up." Her voice cracked, and Maverick knew that even though she seemed cheerful, this whole experience had had an impact on her.

"So, they pulled you out, and they've been taking care of you ever since."

Nash's face came into view. "She's been here ever since, too."

Bailey blushed. "Of course, I'd be here."

Then he remembered her contract and her singing, and he hoped she wasn't missing something big 'cause he'd done something so dumb as to get kicked by a bull. If he hadn't thought he'd won... He moaned and blinked again.

"Oh, of course." Her beautiful eyes stared down into his. "Maverick, you won. And not just won, you beat your own record by so much no one will ever break it again, including you, I'm afraid."

He grinned. At least his mouth worked. Then he moaned. Why couldn't he speak? He cleared his throat and tried to form words.

"Ah, we aren't really sure about your lack of speech. We are hopeful it isn't a stroke or a sign of brain damage."

The seriousness of that possibility descended on him like a bale of hay.

The doctor came in just then, followed by the voices of the twins, and the small, happy voice of Gracie Faith.

He smiled again. "Hello."

"Hey! He spoke!" Gracie jumped up on the bed and peered down into his face as if she'd done it a hundred times. "And his eyes are open!" She studied him. "Hi, Maverick."

"Hi, angel girl." His words sounded muffled, but at least they made sense.

"Did you hear you won?"

"I did."

"Just like me. We can show everyone our ribbons together."

Something about that made him happier than a pig in mud. And he wished he could say so, but his throat was so dry, his tongue so thick, and his words garbled enough that he didn't dare attempt anything more than simple phrases.

The doctor's gentle hands started detaching the neck brace and the wires holding up his arms. "I want you to be very careful and follow my instructions to the letter."

"Okay." Maverick tried to stem the fear that surfaced every few breaths. He focused on the people in the room. Bailey and Gracie acted like they belonged. No one was talking about her running off to do tours. She'd come to see him.

The doctor gently lowered his head back down on the pillow. "Now I want you to try and turn your head. Once to the right."

Maverick successfully passed all the tests the doctor put him through and at last was sitting up in bed.

Bailey smiled, but he could see the worry lines, the stress she'd been feeling. He reached for her hand.

Gracie sat up against his side, making herself comfortable around the IV tubes without a care in the world.

Nash, Decker, and Dylan stood at the end of the bed.

"How long have I been out?"

They all looked at Bailey. "Just a few days."

"How many is a few?"

"Your speech is working better."

He waited.

"Okay, fine. You were out five days. They weren't sure if they could revive you, and because you weren't responsive, no one knew if you'd be paralyzed or not." Tears filled her eyes. "It's been rough, but we are so glad you're back."

"I'm sorry." Without permission, his own tears fell. Embarrassed, he tried to wipe them away.

Nash shook his head. "Don't worry about it. The doc said you'd be weepy for no reason."

Maverick chuckled. "Where's Mama?"

"She's resting. She wouldn't leave your side until we told her Bailey had you taken care of."

"Yeah, my mama wouldn't leave either." Gracie's eyes were large and serious. Maverick knew there was more going on with her statement.

"And was that hard for you?"

She nodded. "I had to go back home." She snuggled closer. "I wanted to stay too."

"Well, I'm happy you got to sleep in a comfortable bed." He lifted his eyes to Bailey's. "Thanks."

She nodded.

The guys joked with him some more, and the more he talked, the more comfortable his speech became. Until he felt almost normal, just tired. His brothers left with promises to bring back Mama. Gracie jumped down and ran with them after they offered her ice cream. And at last, Maverick was alone with Bailey.

She climbed up and sat next to him on the bed. Her fingers ran through his hair. "It's a good thing you broke your own record 'cause I don't think you're getting back up on a bull again." Her voice hitched like she was delivering bad news.

"That's the best news I've heard so far."

"Is it?"

"Oh yeah. Bailey, I couldn't stand another minute of

that lonely road. No one there at night, no one to see my success, nothing but one show after another." He almost said, "I'm ready to come home." But was he? Home wasn't where he wanted to be, either, if Bailey wasn't there.

She snuggled in closer. "I get that." She yawned and then pulled the blankets up around her, turning on her side. In moments, she was asleep.

Tears fell again as he thought of her pain and her apparent exhaustion. He stayed as still as possible so he didn't disturb her, and when the nurse came in to check on him, he shooed her out and shook his head. She smiled and gave them some time.

As he studied Bailey's sleeping form, he hoped that no matter what came next in their lives, they'd be able to do it together.

Chapter 23

The stress of the past week finally caught up to Bailey. It hit her like a truck barreling down the highway, and she couldn't keep her eyes open. She knew Maverick was next to her—she felt his solid rhythmic breathing beside her—but she couldn't even stay awake to enjoy him. He was safe. He was healthy. He would recover. That's all she needed to know before she let her body shut down.

When she awoke, it was to quiet whispers at Maverick's other side. Mama had come back, and she was laying into Maverick like Bailey'd never heard.

"She's done everything for you, son. Took over when you left, was worried sick for you while caring for her own daughter. If that's not proving she's in it for the long haul, I don't know what is. And besides, you're gonna need her. I won't be around forever. Someone's gotta be Mama, and do you think you can find anyone else the guys will respect? What about when they start bringing in their wives and their kids. Someone's gotta keep track of all that nonsense.

"I just wanna rest. I wanna sit on the porch and love on

my grandkids. At least she brought me one of those. Not a single son of mine has even thought about such a thing. Well, besides you, of course, and that isn't your fault. But she's yours now. She is. Can't you see that? That child loves you. And there isn't a contract in the world that's gonna take either of them away from you. If you don't grab hold of this chance and love her like she deserves, I hope your dad comes back from the grave to give you the talking-to you deserve."

Bailey tried not to, but she couldn't help a little laugh and then another. And then Maverick started shaking beside her, and the two of them were laughing like they didn't have a care in the world. Mama stood crossing her arms and looking none too pleased.

"I don't find any of this mess funny."

Bailey sat up and came around the bed. "Oh, Mama, I love you like my own mother. Truer and more important words were never spoken by any woman." She winked over her shoulder at Maverick. "But there's a couple things I gotta say. And one of them is there's no way I could ever do anything for this family half as well as you've already done it. But if you're offering me a position in the Dawson family lineup, I'll take it."

"Wait, what?" Maverick opened his mouth.

"Well, sure." Bailey grinned and then shook her head. "I'm just kidding—a little."

Maverick's face turned completely serious, and she saw the proposal on his lips. Maybe, at last, they could do this again, the right way.

Mama leaned over and kissed his forehead. "You think long and hard about what I said."

"I could never forget a word of it."

"That's a good boy. Because I don't want to be getting after you again. You're old enough to not need these talks anymore."

She found her way back to her seat at the side of the bed. "The doctor came in while you were sleeping, Bailey, and he said that tomorrow, as long as Maverick keeps improving, he can make his way back home." She held up a finger. "To bed rest."

"Oh, that's great news."

"So you can clear out of his room, or we can put him someplace else. Or you can stay in there with him for all I care."

"What!" Bailey felt her face go crimson. "I'll be just fine moving to the guest bedroom."

"You been sleeping in my bed?"

"You don't need to smile so big about it."

"He's just imagining how good his pillows are gonna smell."

It was Maverick's turn to blush crimson. And Bailey laughed. "Oh, it's so good things are getting back to normal."

The day and night passed quickly, and everyone else went home except for Bailey. She pulled the truck up to the outpatient door and helped the nurse load him into the back seat.

"I'm fine. I can climb into my own truck."

"We're just being careful so you don't pass out on the pavement."

He rolled his eyes but submitted to the hospital rules. When at last he shut the truck door and Bailey pulled out of the parking lot, he let the relief wash over him. "Let's go home."

"Yes sir."

But she didn't take him straight to the highway. Instead, she made her way through downtown Fort Worth. They pulled up alongside the Cowtown Coliseum at a red light.

"What are we doing?" he asked.

"Just looking."

He stared out the window. The truck moved forward, and signs for Billy Bob's flashed in neon. Bailey pointed at the signs. "See that place?"

"The dance place?"

"Yep. I sang there once."

"You did?"

"Yes, and I thought I saw your truck out back. That's the first night I thought I might be brave enough to come back."

"Oh yeah, why's that?"

"'Cause all I could think of was running to you and jumping in your arms. I knew if I could feel that again, I'd be okay."

His eyes held pain, and she felt it in her core.

"And then I felt the same thing when you were lying there with your eyes closed, not responding to anything we were saying. I knew that if I could just see your eyes open and feel your arms around me again, everything would be okay."

Her eyes stared into his through the rearview mirror. He looked shaken. "I know what you mean."

"I'm not gonna sign the contract."

"What! Bailey—"

She shook her head. "You think I want to be that lonely person traveling from state to state, doing a concert tour all by myself?"

He looked away. "But what if you need to try?"

"I don't."

"What if all you did was record an album?"

"It's never all you do. They're gonna want a tour to sell the album." Her mind was made up.

He nodded. Then he grimaced.

"What? Are you in pain?" She heard her own anxious tone and didn't care how overprotective she sounded.

"A little."

"I'm sorry. Let's wait to talk about this stuff until you're settled back in and rested."

They drove the rest of the way joking lightly about the passing landscape, about Texas, even about Billy Bob's.

"So you sang there?" Maverick looked impressed, and she had to laugh.

"Yes, I did. Would you have been at the stage, reaching for my hand?"

"Did people do that?"

She smiled at the jealousy in his expression. "We both know I wasn't a big sensation. It was one gig. And I felt lucky to open for another band."

He nodded.

"You didn't answer the question. Would you have been at the stage reaching for my hand?"

"Yes, and backstage, and in your dressing room."

She smiled. "That would have been nice."

"We can still do that."

She didn't answer.

At last, they pulled into his front yard, and Gracie Faith came running out. "Daddy!"

Maverick sucked in a breath.

She pounded on his door, and when he opened it, she

jumped in the truck and threw her arms around his neck. "I'm so glad you're back."

His eyes found Bailey's.

And she didn't know what to say. There was too much goodness in that scene for her to even know how to handle it. This was home. No matter where they went, this, right here, was home.

"This is all I need." Maverick scooted out, trying to hop down with Gracie wrapped around his waist.

They made their way into the house. It smelled delicious. "Your mama is a saint."

"She's your mama, too. More yours than mine, sounded like, last time we chatted."

They both laughed again about the talking-to she'd laid on him in the hospital.

They relaxed with family—all the brothers were home again. Bailey watched Maverick, and as soon as she noticed his fatigue taking over, she stood at his side and offered to help him up the stairs.

And it was further evidence to his exhaustion that he didn't moan about her babying him or complain that he knew how to walk in his own house.

As they neared his bedroom door, she had to wonder if maybe there was another reason he wasn't complaining.

She laughed to herself as the door opened. His huge mahogany bed, with fresh new sheets, looked more inviting than ever.

"Wanna come in for a while?" He wiggled his eyebrows, and she laughed.

"I'm here to put you to bed, mister."

"You heard my mother. She's given up on her house rules for you. Now that's something."

Bailey shook her head. She knew Mama considered them as good as married and was just waiting for the wedding. "I don't think she's given up on God's rules though."

Maverick sat on his bed, leaning back against the headboard. "Let's talk for a minute." He scooted more toward the middle and patted the spot next to him.

She snuggled up against him. "I've imagined moments like this one for years."

"Me too." He kissed the top of her head. "I got something to say. And this might not be the most romantic way to do this, but just remember back on the first time I asked you, on top of the water tower with the sun setting behind us."

Her heart leapt. She held his hand in her own, tracing lines up and down his fingers.

"I want to marry you, Bailey. Really marry you. As in, you walk down the aisle, I meet you in front of the preacher, and we say 'I do.'"

She winced a little, but she knew he needed reassurance.

He held up his hand. "I want to grow old with you, Bailey. I want you in this spot on the bed every night for the rest of your life."

She turned to look up into his face.

"But what do you want?" His kind eyes, his open, caring expression made this one of the most special moments of their relationship.

She tried to think of a way to express herself that he could fully trust. "I want to finally walk down that aisle. I want to be yours every day from now until forever. But..."

"But?" He lifted her chin so he could study her eyes.

"But this isn't my spot."

He tilted his head in question.

"Nope." She leaned over and pointed to his other side. "That's my spot."

"Whoa now, I've been sleeping in that spot for years."

"Well, me too, so what are you gonna do about it?"

"Is this a deal-breaker?"

"It might be."

He seemed to give it some real serious thought, then he wrapped his arms around her and rolled her over to that spot, covering her body with the length of his own. "Then how about we share?" His eyes were laughing, teasing, tempting, but as he waited for her response, they darkened. He adjusted his position so that he rested on his arms. "This is probably a little too nice for the kind of conversation we're having, but I'll just wait here until I get an answer."

"About sharing our spot?"

"Yes, that, and other things I'm about to ask."

"You're gonna ask right here?"

"Why not? I like it." The twinkle of enjoyment on his face made her grin.

"We can share."

"What else do you want, Bailey? Do you want to sing? To travel? Do you want to stay here and help run the ranch? Do you love Willow Creek? Me?" The last, hopeful lift of his voice warmed her heart. He knew she loved him, but she didn't blame him for his insecurity in that area. She vowed to spend the rest of her days trying to wipe it away.

"I told you the truth. I still have the contract, and I look at it every now and then, but I don't want a big singing career anymore. I think I might be happy singing here in Willow Creek and at our local county fair."

He nodded and kissed her forehead. Then he lifted himself up and fell to his knees at the side of the bed. "Bailey, I just can't wait any longer. Will you marry me? We'll figure out all the rest later."

She rolled off and knelt down beside him. He turned to her. She lifted a finger and ran it along his forehead. "I love you, Maverick. Whatever we do, let's do it together. Yes, I will marry you as soon as we possibly can."

"Praise be."

She laughed. "What?"

"Oh, come here." He pulled her close and kissed her like he meant it, short, meaningful pressure. Then, as he continued, the kisses slowed and lingered, his love pouring into each one until Bailey hardly knew how to respond, so full of Maverick and his love and this beautiful feeling between them. Her fingers rose up into his hair, and she pulled his face closer as he rolled her down onto the carpet beside the bed. Then, with his hand on her hip, he said, "I love you, too, Bailey. Stay with me." He rested his head back. "I'm exhausted, but I don't want you to leave."

"Right here on the floor?"

"Sure." His eyes closed, and his breathing steadied.

"No, wake up." She nudged him. "Let's get you back in bed."

Barely coherent, he crawled back up onto her side of the bed and closed his eyes. "Stay," he mumbled.

So she did. She curled up next to him, wrapping her arms as far around his waist as they would go, pressed her cheek into his back, and stayed until he fell asleep.

Chapter 24

Bailey sat in the same bride's room at the same church as the first time she'd planned to marry Maverick, the day she should have stayed.

But looking back, if she'd stayed, she would never have known just how precious her life was at this moment. She didn't quite forgive what she'd done, but she knew she'd get there. How could she keep from herself what God gave? The sweet peace of her prayers had been her greatest solace and her strength. If God loved her, maybe she could love herself, even with her messed up past.

The contract to record an album sat on her dressing table. Why did she bring it with her? She could not even venture to guess. But seeing it now, it felt important that she didn't have even a twinge of longing. Nothing that paper offered was even half as wonderful as the life she would lead with Maverick and Gracie in Willow Creek. She knew that now.

She stood in front of the mirror. Her mom had already come and left. She was likely sitting in the front row with her father. By now, Maverick was standing at the head of the congregation, each of his brothers in a line beside him.

A small knock at the door made her smile.

"Mama?"

She opened it. "Gracie Faith, you look beautiful." Her little dress was white like Bailey's, and it flowed to the floor. She carried matching flowers, and her eyes lit with so much love and excitement. They filled Bailey with a whole new happiness, all for Gracie. "Such a beautiful girl, inside and out."

Her eyes widened. "You look beautiful, too. Daddy is not gonna know what to say."

Bailey laughed. "I'm so happy to hear you calling him Daddy. How did that come about, anyway?"

She twirled in her dress, making it poof out all around her. "'Cause I wanted him for my daddy."

Simple enough. Bailey reached for her hand. "You ready for this?"

"Uh huh."

"You know it's something special to be a Dawson."

"Yup." Her face crinkled. "And it's something special to just be us, too."

Bailey's eyes threatened to tear up. "You are so right. It's something special just to be you."

Gracie nodded.

The two of them walked down the hallway of the church to the back double doors and then nodded to the attendants.

As the doors opened, the music started, and she and Gracie walked down the aisle together, side by side. The church was packed. Everyone from Willow Creek had come out to see them finally get hitched. Those who couldn't fit inside were lined up outside along the front. As she walked down the aisle, she passed her fellow teachers at the middle school, friends from high school, even Tiff and her friends were there, and they'd brought dates. Perfect. She kept walking. Her parents smiled their wonderful, accepting love, strengthening her yet again. Then Mama Dawson, her eyes full of support, reached her hand out. Bailey gave it a squeeze. A whole line of brothers, each one strong, true, and handsome, grinned at her. When her eyes met Maverick's, she picked up her pace, racing against the beat of the music.

He moved to take her hand and led her up two stairs to stand at his side. Gracie Faith stood behind her. "In a hurry?"

"Aren't you?"

"Absolutely."

Epilogue

Epilogue *Five Years Later*

Bailey and Maverick stood in front of their bathroom mirrors getting ready for the Dawson Ranch event of the year. Maverick turned to face her. "Can you straighten this?" His bow tie never sat right without her help.

She worked her magic, bouncing a little to a song on the radio. Then the announcer came on. "And now for our own local favorite, Bailey Dawson."

Maverick leaned forward and kissed her until her toes curled. "And they don't even know about the best parts of you."

"Oh, hush." She always felt her face heat when their conversation turned that way.

One more dab of lipstick to replace what he'd kissed away, and she reached for his hand. "You ready? Your fans await."

"*Your* fans, more like." He studied her. "And no, come to think of it, I'm not ready." He pulled her close again. Her long, sleek dress draped against his tux. "I'm needing a little something first."

"Oh yeah?" She stood up on her tiptoes.

"Yeah." He covered her mouth with his, kissing off every bit of pink lipstick she'd just applied, but she loved every second. When they'd finally finished, and she'd reapplied lipstick, readjusted her dress, and tidied up her hair, they made their way down the stairs to the Dawson Ranch dinner and demonstration for all of their sponsors and partners.

Each of the brothers was there with a date, representing their own business offshoots of the Dawson brand. The whole town came to support. And most importantly, their own children. Mama had gotten them there early, to sit at the side table, out of the way but well within sight and reach.

"You know what, Mrs. Dawson?"

"What's that?"

"We've got it pretty dang good." He pressed his lips to her forehead, and they made their way to the front of the room to welcome their guests, everyone clapping in welcome, but no one louder than their daughter, Gracie, and their son, Gunner.

Read all books by Sophia Summers

JOIN HERE for all new release announcements, giveaways and the insider scoop of books on sale.

Her Billionaire Royals Series:
The Heir
The Crown
The Duke
The Duke's Brother
The Prince
The American
The Spy
The Princess

Read all the books in The Swoony Sports Romances
Hitching the Pitcher
Falling for Centerfield
Charming the Shortstop
Snatching the Catcher
Flirting with First

Read all books by Sophia Summers

Kissing on Third

Vacation Billionaires
Holiday Romance

Her Billionaire Cowboys Series:
Her Billionaire Cowboy
Her Billionaire Protector
Her Billionaire in Hiding
Her Billionaire Christmas Secret
Her Billionaire to Remember

Her Love and Marriage Brides Series
The Bride's Secret
The Bride's Cowboy
The Bride's Billionaire

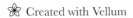

Made in the USA
San Bernardino, CA
08 June 2020

72864195R00135